THE RELUCTANT

COURIER

Pam Stevens

About the Author

Pam Stevens, the author of "The Reluctant Courier", is a remarkable individual who has accomplished numerous feats throughout her life. With over 33 years of marriage and a successful business career in a male-dominated industry, Pam Stevens has demonstrated her perseverance and tenacity. Growing up on a farm and learning how to train horses at a young age, she has always been passionate about pursuing her interests.

Pam Stevens started her writing career after the age of 40 after she worked for the Horseman's News as a photographer and writer. After years of reading, she realized she had a knack for writing and began to pursue it further. Despite the loss of her mother last year, she pushed herself to publish her first book.

Acknowledgements

Thank you to my husband and kids who put up with me saying, "Wait a minute I have to finish this." Without all of your encouragement and support this book would never have become a reality

Dedication

To Mom & Dad - Thank you for encouraging me to follow my dream, you are both gone now but I know you are looking down and saying "Finally!"

Contents

CHAPTER ONE

Sandra Stanford sat in a small dingy cafe drinking coffee and gazing thoughtfully out into the darkness through the dirty front window. She was a petite girl of twenty-five, with short brown hair that curled uncontrollably around her small face giving her a pixyish appearance. Her large, Irish green eyes held a hint of sadness in their depths, as if she had been deeply hurt in the not-too-distant past, but her ready smile and lighthearted attitude appeared so genuine that the sadness was rarely noticed and then only by the very astute.

Why did I stop here, she wondered idly, grimacing after taking a sip of coffee, this place not only has rotten coffee, but it's filthy too? Oh well, what can one expect to find at four in the morning, especially when that someone is too lazy to fix herself a cup of coffee?

There were only two other people in the cafe, one was a bleached blond waitress, who might have been at least attractive with about a pound less makeup and naturally colored hair, she had decided silently. The other, probably a truck driver, from the truck outside that she had noticed when coming in, was definitely not her idea of an enticing individual. The type that acted as though he was God's gift to women, even though he was dirty, unshaven, and in general unkempt. They sat talking softly to one another at the end of the counter in the back of the cafe, each seemingly completely absorbed in the other. It takes all kinds, Sandra thought humorously, as she turned back to the window.

Sandra, known as Sandi by her friends, noticed as a bus pulled up and stopped across the street from the cafe, apparently letting someone off. A stooped figure of a man was left standing alone on the far side of the road when it pulled away a few moments later. She hadn't noticed any other homes or buildings, so she decided the cafe must be his destination. Then she wondered why anyone would want to leave the comparative comfort of the bus for this flea-bitten hole in the wall.

Curiously she sat watching the man as he glanced around before walking toward the cafe. Suddenly a car appeared out of what seemed to be nowhere, its lights were out and it was speeding straight at him! Sandi started for the cafe door without even thinking, she only knew that someone was about to be run down by an idiotic driver. Like a bad dream, everything seemed to shift into slow motion, everything that is, except the car. She wanted to scream at him, warn him, yet she knew that it was already too late. He saw the car and tried to jump clear but it simply swerved into him. There was a horribly dull thud, then nothing but the roar of the car's engine as it disappeared into the inky blackness.

The man lay on the far side of the road, he was moaning when Sandi reached his side. She knelt down placing her hand gently on his arm, "Please, don't try to talk, just lie still while I get help."

The others were starting toward the cafe door now, having been in the back and absorbed in one another, they had missed seeing the reason for Sandi's abrupt exit.

"No! Wait!" The man spoke softly to Sandi; his voice was surprisingly strong considering his appearance. In the dim light from the cafe windows, she watched as he licked his pale lips with the tip of his tongue before shoving an envelope into her hand. Then he spoke again, his voice becoming weaker with the effort. "Take this protect it with your life must get to Steven Hoyt... no one else... Could mean war please," his voice was only a weak whisper now and she had to lean closer to even hear him, "Congressman Washington... Tell him to look..." The rest was only a rattle in his throat. A thin line of blood trickled from his mouth and another from his nose as his head fell to one side.

The two from the cafe were cautiously crossing the street, Sandi heard the truck driver ask what was going on as she lifted the leg of her pants and slipped the mysterious envelope down inside her western boot. Then she turned to them, the man's last words racing through her mind.

"One of you call an ambulance, this man's been hit by a car, I think he's still alive, but just barely." She knew her voice didn't sound quite normal, but it was the best she could do under the circumstances.

Instead of doing as she said, both ran over and peered down at the stricken man. The truck driver turned to Sandi after a moment, "See if you can find a blanket, I'll stay with him. Linda," he turned to the waitress, "Why don't you go call an ambulance like the lady suggested." It sounded more like an order than a question.

"I've had some training in nursing; I'll try to help..."

That was all Sandi heard of the conversation as she hurried to her 'rig' for a blanket, glad to have someone else take charge of the situation. Her head was spinning with thoughts of the injured man's plea and the accident, which probably wasn't an accident at all, she realized, but an attempted murder instead. Sandi's 'rig' consisted of an old bus converted into a camper and horse trailer in one, she was a professional rodeo contestant so it served as home most of the time.

Grabbing the first blanket that was handy and starting to return, she saw that the waitress and truck driver still seemed to be arguing over who should go call for help, and who should stay with the poor man. She abruptly changed directions and went into the cafe to phone for help instead. Waiting on the line a few moments later the thought crossed her mind that the two outside were certainly turning into a worthless lot in an emergency, arguing at a time like this!

Hanging up the phone after giving the operator all the information she could, she turned toward the door with the blanket feeling guilty for not taking it out first, but she hadn't thought that the phone call would take all that much time. "The poor guy's probably in shock by now, if he's still alive," she muttered angrily. Of course, if those two hadn't been acting so scatterbrained one of them would have done the calling, she thought. Or maybe I'm just overreacting, I've probably been reading too many of those thrillers, and with what that guy said I'm the one who's acting a little scatterbrained.

It was only a few minutes until the police arrived but to Sandi, it seemed an eternity. The man was still lying where she had left him, but a quick glance at the others was all it took to tell her something was decidedly, fishy. Though the light was still dim, it was enough for her to see the truck driver lying off to one side, his hands apparently either tied or handcuffed behind him. And the waitress, while kneeling over the injured man, was pointing a gun straight at her! The injured-man's coat lay open, Sandi was sure it had been closed before, had he been searched?

Oh Lordy, what now, she asked herself, freezing in her tracks. I've had a bad feeling about these two ever since I laid eyes on them, but I never expected this. I guess I'll just have to play this thing by ear and see what happens, at least the police are on their way, I hope.

"Did he say anything to you?" The waitress demanded, interrupting her thoughts.

I wonder what the heroine in the book I'm reading would do in a case like this. Of course, just bluff her way out of it, acting like a dumb blond. Small problem, I'm not blond and I've never been very good at poker...

"I believe I asked you a question," the waitress interrupted her thoughts again. She stood up, still brandishing the gun, and took a step toward her as if she meant to use it.

Sandi shook her head and blinked her eyes, hoping the image would leave, but it didn't. "I beg your pardon, but I seem to find all this is a little unreal. A man lies dying at your feet and you're worried about whether or not he said anything to me, you can't be serious!" She was rather pleased with how well her attempt to sound both incredulous and enraged at the same time had turned out, especially considering that total terror was much closer to her real state of mind.

The gun wavered, but it wasn't lowered. "There is nothing more you or anyone else can do for him, he's dead. My name is Barbara Parker, I work for the FBI, now will you answer my question?"

Sandi paused, thinking how nice and easy it would be to turn the envelope over to this girl here and now and be done with it, but the man's whispered words "no one else" came floating back to play a haunting melody in her mind. "After all," she thought, "how am I to know if she really is whom she says, even if she showed me some ID, which she hasn't. It can be forged, and the man lying on the ground is proof that murder isn't too high a price to pay for what she wants."

"You're taking your sweet time in answering. This happens to be rather important, did he, or did he not, say anything to you?" The impatience in Barbara's voice seemed to hang in the cold early morning air.

"Sorry," Sandi spoke at last, trying to decide just how to answer, "but I don't happen to care for guns, especially when they're pointing at me."

"Then answer the damn question!"

Sandi shrugged, "I don't guess there's any harm, but I want the name of your superior, I want him to know how you treat everyday citizens who are just trying to help." Barbara sighed with impatience. "He didn't say anything that I could understand." That was at least partially true, she really didn't know what he was talking about. "He was moaning, I would guess from pain, when I got to him. I know I would be if a car had just hit me. And I seriously doubt that I would feel particularly conversational either. Incidentally, I called the police, they and an ambulance will be here any minute. You and he," she nodded at the trucker, "seemed to have other interests." Sandi figured that it couldn't hurt for this Barbara, or Linda, or whoever she

8

was, to know that the police were on their way, especially if she had anything unhealthy in mind for her.

She must have finally said something right; Barbara lowered the gun before answering. "There's more at stake here than one man's life. Why don't we throw that blanket over him and go inside out of the cold until the police arrive? If I hadn't had my hands full with that creep," she motioned at the truck driver, "I might have been able to stop you." Noticing Sandi's startled look at her last comment she smiled, and added, "Oh, not that they shouldn't have been called, eventually, it's just that the agency isn't going to like the police asking a lot of questions, like are we involved with this?"

"Well, aren't you?" Sandi asked boldly, turning back to the cafe after laying the blanket over the dead man."

"Let's just say that what the agency is, or isn't involved in, is not necessarily public knowledge, not yet anyway. I want to ask you some questions before the police get here, will you cooperate?"

"If I don't, will I wind up in the same condition as him?" Sandi asked, indicating the trucker who was now stumbling across the street in front of them.

"Very likely." Barbara replied dryly.

"Then I guess I cooperate, just what is it you wish to know?" She was scared, for the first time in her life, she was really frightened. Never in her life or even her wildest dreams had she ever been in a situation like this, yet she knew that she had to keep from showing it, that she had to somehow out think and out maneuver this woman.

During the remaining time until the police arrived, Sandi answered Barbara's questions in the backroom of the cafe while Barbara changed into a simple business suit and removed the excess makeup she was wearing. Completely unknown to Sandi there had been someone else in the café all along, the owner. He had been staying in the backroom, apparently at Barbara's request. By the time she had finished listening to Barbara thank him for his cooperation and answering all of her questions, she was beginning to regret ever seeing the man get off the bus. For that matter, Sandi berated herself, why did I have to push on and drive all night to ride in some stupid rodeo, it's not as though it's the only one in the world. Besides, if I stopped somewhere and slept all night, I still could have gotten there in time to ride. Me and my insomnia, I seem to have really landed in it this time!

"Need I remind you that you promised your full cooperation, Mrs. Stanford?" Barbara asked as the police pulled up in front of the cafe. "I don't want you to refute anything I tell the police."

Sandi smiled sweetly, "I seriously doubt that the police would believe a mere citizen over a FBI agent, so you have nothing to worry about. I just want to get this whole thing over with so I can get back on the road. Just between the two of us, this whole scene is not exactly my cup of tea!"

Moments later, Sandi listened to Barbara's explanation to the police of her presence. "No, the agency isn't involved officer, I just happened to be here at the wrong time, that's all. The trucker was attempting to lift the guy's valuables, so I cuffed him. Maybe you should check him out. Here's my card, if you need me for anything else I can be reached at that number."

If it weren't for the fact that Sandi had the distinct impression she was in a league way over her head she might have given in to her temptation to expose Barbara Parker's and the FBI's interest in the man and his death. But she couldn't see that it would help her get the envelope delivered, and her chances didn't look all that promising anyway. After all, one man had died trying, and he probably knew more about this game than she even dreamed of learning. The best thing she could do, she decided, was to answer the police officer's questions and get the hell out of there, preferably without attracting anymore attention to herself.

"You're Mrs. Stanford, is that correct?" She nodded, "could you tell me what you saw please?" The officer in charge asked her.

"I was sitting, looking out the window of the cafe, when he got off the bus. I saw the car come from that direction," she turned and pointed down the road before continuing, "its lights were out... it just ran him down." Her voice wavered as she remembered the horrifying scene.

"Did you see what sort of car it was, the license number, anything that might help us identify the vehicle? I realize this isn't easy for you Mrs. Stanford, seeing a man killed and all, but anything you can recall might help us find the crazy who did it."

She shook her head, "I couldn't see the license... it was a late model, it looked kind of like a Chevy, but I'm not sure, so many look alike now. It was a dark color; I'd say either midnight blue or black. I'm sorry I wish I could be of more help, but it all happened so fast."

"I understand, we thank you for your cooperation, I won't detain you any longer." He turned to another patrolman, "Sure seems strange, the guy not having any ID on him, money, yeah, but no papers. Coroner on the way?"

Sandi wondered if she looked as guilty as she felt, it wasn't as though she had done anything wrong, more like omitted, but still, she felt as though she had somehow committed a crime. Her only hope was that everyone would chalk her nervousness up to being a witness to a murder, not to carrying around some important information that could start a war. One was bad enough without the other, and the combination was enough to put her on the verge of hysteria. Only the thought of getting caught and ending up dead kept her from falling completely to pieces.

A faint light showed in the East, a new day was dawning as Sandi left the cafe. She wondered what else it held in store for her; so far it hadn't been particularly pleasant.

CHAPTER TWO

Sandi glanced nervously in her rear view mirror again; the car was still behind her. If that guy is following me, she thought, he certainly isn't trying very hard to hide it. Which probably means he is either just watching me to see what I'm going to do, or, he's trying to scare me. I'm glad he doesn't know what a fantastic job he is doing with the latter.

Having no idea just how many, if any, followers she had, Sandi had decided to try a few tricks. After all, she had concluded, I haven't read all those thrilling murder and spy mysteries for nothing. I just hope it works in real life as well as it does in fiction.

All she had to do was convince anyone watching her that she did not have that all important envelope or know anything about it. This was supposed to be accomplished by traveling away from her, final destination of Washington D.C. First a scenic trip to Valley Forge, whether or not it led anyone off the track, she didn't know, but seeing the place where so many men had suffered and died for their country certainly strengthened her resolve to deliver the envelope, regardless, of the personal consequences. Then it was on to the town of Wilkes-Barre to ride in a rodeo that was to start that evening. By then, hopefully, anyone entertaining the thought that she was involved would have given up on the idea after seeing her proceed as though nothing had happened. And then, at that point, she would be able to deliver the envelope to Congressman Steven Hoyt. It all sounded good in theory, but Sandi was a died-in-the-wool believer in Murphy's Law.

She would have been delighted to know that she had put a definite crook in a few individuals' plans by not taking the road straight to Washington. In fact, her entire caravan of followers found her actions to say the least a little confusing. None, however, gave up the chase, deciding the prize, if she had it, was much too valuable for hasty conclusions.

"We're almost there girl," Sandi spoke to her dog, Bubbles, lying quietly beside her, "let's see, a right turn here at the light, and there it is, straight ahead." The only acknowledgment she received was a bored sigh and a light thumping sound from the dog's tail. "You're a real live wire today, aren't you?" She added, reaching down and scratching Bubbles behind one ear.

15

Sandi pulled the bus into the parking area designated for contestants, greeting other circuit riders she knew while looking for a place to park. Sam, a young wrangler who worked for the stock contractor, waved her to a stop.

"How ya been, Sweetheart?" He asked, jumping onto the step of the bus and grabbing the window ledge.

"Fine, just fine," Sandi replied dryly, with a forced smile, thinking she should become an accomplished liar by the time this escapade was finished, because she certainly didn't feel fine. Anxiety from the responsibility of carrying an envelope, the contents of which at least one man had died for, coupled with lack of sleep were beginning to take their toll.

A piece of paper fell from Sam's hand down the inside of the door. "Don't reach for it!" He whispered, "Just act normal." Then he stepped back saying loudly, "Good luck, tonight."

"Thanks Sam," was all she could manage to get out as she put the bus in gear and drove forward leaving Sam wondering what had happened to her in the week since he had seen her last.

Sandi found a parking place before picking up the note with shaking hands. "'Act normal', right! This is ridiculous, now I'm scared of a silly piece of paper?" Her hands still shook; she didn't know Sam very well, but well enough to tell her that something was wrong. He had never called her Sweetheart or jumped on her bus, or written her notes. The simple fact was, their longest conversation had probably contained a half-a-dozen civilities, 'Hi', 'How are things', etc., etc.

There's a man here looking for you. Tall, blue eyes, blond hair, gray business suit. Something about him struck me as bad news, hope I'm wrong. He offered me $200 to point you out, told him I didn't even know you. If you need help you've plenty of it here.

Sam

Someone must have figured out where I was headed and decided to have a welcoming party. Maybe I should try to make it to Washington. No! Now don't panic and do something stupid, she admonished herself. The best way to get out of a situation like this is to keep a cool head and think faster than you opponent. Now that's royal, I've never been in a situation like this, just how does one go about out thinking an adversary they've never even seen? This spy game or whatever it is, is just not fair. I don't even know how to think along those lines. Besides, she shuddered, I'm scared, and these people will kill to get what I have!

She was so completely engrossed in her thoughts that she failed to notice the happenings around her until a loud voice yelled her name and someone banged on the side door of the rig causing her to jump like a scared rabbit. She recognized Joey's impatient voice when he yelled again.

"Hey Sandi, are you in there? What the hell are you doing, sleeping?"

Not a bad idea, she thought, desperately trying to pull her frayed nerves together before opening the door. The Sandi that opened the door held very little resemblance to the one Joey knew, her unusually pale face with deep dark circles under her eyes left him shocked nearly speechless.

Joey was one of Sandi's many admirers, and probably the most faithful of all. They had met at the Calgary Stampede about a year earlier and only because of his relentless pursuit of her had they become good friends. Much to his dismay though, that was as far as it had gone. Sandi, he discovered, was an easy person to meet, but practically impossible to know. In all the time they had spent together he had ascertained only sketchy details of

18

her past, none of which he was overly positive about. She had been married twice, once when she was very young, .he assumed that it had ended in divorce. And again to a race car driver which had ended with his death in a fiery crash nearly two years back. To his knowledge she had never let anyone get really close to her since. It was only because of his knowledge of her aversion to talk about herself or anything disturbing her that he bit off an exclamation of surprise at her worn appearance.

Sandi opened the door with feelings of great relief, here was someone on whom she, could depend on to help her, someone she could lean on. But before the thought of pouring the whole story out to Joey had been completed in her mind another shoved it out. The man had said 'no one else, it was bad enough that she was in this mess without dragging Joey into it too. No, she decided, this is my problem and Joey has nothing to do with it.

They stood staring at one another for a few moments. Joey was every girl's dream of the handsome cowboy. Midnight black hair with a naturally dark complexion naturally from Indian ancestry, his brilliant blue eyes gave a startling effect, one that very few females could resist. Sandi often wondered how she had been able to, and decided that it must be that his devil-may-care attitude left her wondering at the sincerity of his feelings. Besides, she was comfortable with the status quo and didn't really want to become seriously involved with anyone.

"Well, do I pass?" His question sent her thoughts flying in a thousand directions for the second time in less than five minutes. "I'm never sure what you're thinking behind those beautiful green eyes. Did you decide I had the plague and am the last person you wanted to see hanging on your door step, or were you changing your mind about that question I asked you at Tri-State?"

"That would be telling wouldn't it?" She countered, trying to think of a way to get him off the subject of them and explain her totally haggard condition. "My insomnia has been acting up and I haven't slept in over twenty-four hours, and, I have a rodeo to ride in shortly, and, in general I'm not feeling very sociable. How about leaving me alone for awhile?" She hated being that way, but she didn't know what else to do under the circumstances.

"I see, I've got the plague, have I? Well, why don't you go rest, and I'll warm up Rap and get things set up for you?"

Sandi's horse's full name was Rapscallion, he had earned it as a foal for his mischievous pranks, and somehow it had stuck. Probably because he had never outgrown pulling a prank or two whenever the mood struck him and he had a chance.

She smiled in spite of herself, shaking her head in resignation, "I should have known you couldn't take a hint. I really don't feel like resting just yet, but if you won't go away then I guess you may as well make yourself useful."

Sandi was well-liked by both the men and women who rode the rodeo circuit. One clown affectionately called her Sunny instead of Sandi because of what he called her sunny smile and laughter. Joey was seeing a side of her nature he had never seen, one he had never known existed, and it puzzled him, he wanted to remove the hunted look in her eyes, but if she wouldn't tell him what the problem was, he didn't see how he could help her. He just knew that he couldn't just turn his back and walk away.

CHAPTER THREE

Down the highway, a short distance, a tall, blond-haired man in a gray suit leaned superciliously against the side of his car, a shiny midnight blue Caprice. A smaller, unkempt man shifted nervously in front of him. "I tried to get it Boss, really I did, but he didn't have it. You don't think I'd mess up a job this important smaller, unkempt man if I could've helped it do ya? Jeeze, that damn blond nailed me so fast I didn't even know what hit me, I couldn't believe it. But she didn't find the list either, Nash must have stashed it somewhere before you got him. Or he gave it to the little brunette before he kicked off. I just know they didn't find it either," the smaller man whined.

"You know what the penalty is for lousing up. He paused to light a thin cheroot and blow a couple of perfect smoke rings. A cold chill traveled up the spine of the smaller man, he knew, he also knew that there was no place to run, no place to hide that his boss wouldn't find him. He tried to swallow the growing lump in his throat, staying in jail might have postponed it, but it was too late to think of that now, it had really been too late ever since that fateful morning, and maybe even before that, now he was going to die. His boss finally continued, he had enjoyed watching the little man squirm, he liked the feeling of power it gave him, but, he didn't have all day to stand around, there was business to attend to. "The people we work for pay for perfection. In other words, getting caught off guard by some measly dame and winding up in the slammer is not, how should I put it . . . acceptable. In fact, the only reason you're still around is they apparently didn't find that damn list either, just remember, you mess up again and I'll personally take care of you, you understand?"

An unbidden sigh of relief escaped the little man's lips, "Yeah Boss, sure, I won't let ya down." He relaxed some now, he wasn't going to die, he would find that list, and maybe, just maybe, have a little fun in the process. "You want I should get hold of that rodeo chick and find out what she knows? Girl like that, could be real enjoyable getting her to talk?" He smiled maliciously, just the thought of it made him tingle with anticipation.

He remembered the way she had looked at him in the cafe, he'd teach her!

"You stay away from her, I'll take care of her. You backtrack Nash and find out if and where he stashed that list. If he did, you had better find it, first, do I make myself clear?"

"Sure Boss, I told ya, I won't let ya down. "He was disappointed in the girl and some of it showed in his voice.

"There'll be plenty of time for fun and games when this is over. I'll even keep her around for you, consider her a bonus.

Then I can take care of you both at the same time, he added silently. Miles away in an office in Washington three men sat talking despondently. "I don't know what happened Mr. President. Everything seemed to be proceeding as planned. I've had my best people on this from the start, strictest security, everything. Nash wasn't a rookie, I can't see him, even dying, giving that list to some stranger."

"Have you got a better explanation for what happened to it?" Steven Hoyt asked quietly.

"No, damn it, do you think I'd be sitting here if I did, hell no, I'd be out getting it myself!" The first man, Wayne, returned.

"Gentlemen, gentlemen," the President interrupted, "this is getting us nowhere. What I'd like here are some constructive ideas on how to solve our problem. There has been too much time and money put into this project to let it all go to waste."

"I'll have to agree with you there," Steve spoke again. "Wayne, where is this Sandra Stanford now?"

"At the last report from Barbara, she was at some rodeo up in Wilkes-Barre, that's a few hours drive, north of here."

"And you're certain that she isn't involved with the other side?" Steve asked pointedly.

"As certain as we can be under the circumstances.

We've checked her out and as near as we can ascertain she is a normal, law-abiding citizen. She just happened to be in the wrong place at the wrong time. About the only thing I can say is that wherever that list is, they don't have it either. Barbara assured me that she isn't the only one interested in the girl's actions."

"That's something in our favor, but I don't like to think of that girl out there without protection," the President spoke up again.

"I've got two people watching her sir. Course they would step in to help her should the need arise," Wayne replied.

The President shook his head, it. I think."

"I still don't like it…"
"Excuse me," Wayne's secretary interrupted, sticking her head around the office door.

"Yes Vera, what is it?" Wayne motioned her into the room.

"I thought you should be made aware of this latest piece of information on Mrs. Stanford." She handed Wayne a computer readout, before making a hasty retreat back to her office.

Wayne sighed and shook his head, "I don't believe it, just what we need."

"What?" The President Steve both asked in unison.

"The girl's got a damn photographic memory."

"So what, if she doesn't have the list, I fail to see the relevance," the President replied.

"I do," Steve was quick to pick up. "She wouldn't have to do anything more than look at that list and she could reconstruct it anytime she wanted to, for anyone she wanted to.

"But I thought we had decided that she didn't have the list," The President pointed out, still baffled as to what he had missed.

"Correction, we don't think she has it, the key word being - think. But, they may think she does, and if they get a hold of this information, they will pick her up just to be sure one way or the other. If she does have the list or has seen it, they'll find some way of getting her to talk. If not, they'll make her wish she did know something. Either way, she'll probably be dead by this time tomorrow."

"Then we must protect her, bring her here to Washington if necessary", the President decided quickly.

"That's quite a risk, sir," Wayne protested.

"I know it's a risk,

"I know it's a risk, but what isn't nowadays? I can't risk anyone's life unnecessarily."

"My point 'entirely, if we do pick her up, we'll have to give her at least three times the protection we are now. They will be sure she knows something. Hell, we'll probably have to give her a new identity before this is over.

Something I'm not sure she'll be particularly pleased about. And I don't think I need to tell you what could happen if she got hurt, or God forbid, killed, and the press got wind of it. They would have a field day, at your expense, I might add. "

"My expense be damned, there's a girl's life at stake here. We know they have already killed one man, and two agents are missing in the jungle somewhere, probably dead too. Just how long do you think this girl could stand up to their interrogative methods? Steve's right, she'll probably be dead by this time tomorrow if we don't do something. I have to be able to sleep nights whether I'm president or not."

"What if we've been fed bogus info on this girl, what if she's a decoy so we don't believe they have the list," Wayne asked, trying another tack.

"Then we'll have her right here where we can keep an eye on her. We have to check all the other avenues, of course, backtrack Nash, everything," Steve stepped in.

"Okay, let's just say we do decide to bring her here, what makes you so sure she'll go along with it?

From what Barbara told me, this Sandra Stanford is not exactly sweetness and light, in fact, she was downright antagonistic for awhile." Wayne came up with another stumbling block.

"I think I know of a way to get her here, without drawing too much undue attention and with her cooperation.

CHAPTER FOUR

Though women can and often do compete in rodeos male dominated events such as roping and bronc riding, and even bull riding, Sandi preferred the women's event, barrel racing. This event consists of running a clover-leaf course around three barrels in the least possible time, a highly competitive sport requiring both an excellent horse and a great deal of team work between the rider and mount. Rapscallion filled the bill for the horse, he was agile for the quick turns, fast on the straight-aways, and had an infallible love for Sandi, an accomplished equestrian. She had practically grown up on her Grandfather's Quarter horse ranch in California. Though her family had lived several miles from the ranch in an affluent part of the city she had nagged her mother incessantly after school, weekends, and holidays to take her out to the ranch. A recalcitrant child underfoot had never fit into her mother's lifestyle so Sandi had had her way. A fact she had never regretted, though was sure her mother often did.

Not withstanding having been raised around Quarter horses, a breed well known for its ability to work stock and compete successfully in barrel racing, Sandi had always preferred the refinement of Arabians. A preference that had very nearly been her Grandfather's undoing when she finally got up the nerve to voice it two years earlier. His comments on their flightiness and inability to perform, especially in stock work and barrel racing, had sparked her on a stubborn search to find the Arabian that could prove him wrong. Rapscallion had done so, together they had won the coveted tittle, of World Champion Barrel Racer the year before. Of course, now her Grandfather held that it was only because of him that she had done so well, contending that he had known all along that an Arab could do it, after all Quarter horses were indirect descendants of the desert breed. He had just wanted her to come out of her despondency from her husband's death and what better way than to get her angry enough to prove him wrong? She secretly thought he had done the right thing, intentionally or not.

However, this was not Sandi's night, for she placed just out of the money. A lousy end to top off an already lousy day, Sandi thought after hearing her time, a mere two hundredths of a second too slow. Little did she realize, it wasn't over just yet.

"That was definitely not the best ride you've ever made, Sandi. Wouldn't like to tell me your problem would you?" Joey asked, as he rode up next to her while she threaded her way back through the milling crowd of people and horses to her rig.

"Probably lack of shut eye," she answered as lightly as she could, wishing not for the first time that he would go away and leave her alone for a while. The longer he stayed around the more tempted she became to tell him of her plight. She was no longer sure that she was even going to be able to deliver the envelope, on at least six occasions since she arrived at the rodeo she was sure she had seen someone watching her.

"Don't believe it, I've seen you ride, and win, with almost no sleep. But I won't push it, just remember if you need me, I'm available. And Sandi, there aren't any strings attached, just one friend helping another," Joey offered.

"Joey," she murmured emotionally, "thank you, I will..."

"Excuse me, aren't you Sandra Stanford?" A deep voice interrupted her as a hand was laid lightly on her leg.

Sandi felt a chill travel up her leg and through her spine as she summoned a smile and turned toward the speaker. The smile quickly faded when she looked down, however. Blond hair, blue eyes, gray suit, the man Sam warned me about? She asked herself. Sam didn't say exactly why he didn't like the looks of him, but I'll bet I can guess, those eyes remind me of icebergs. She finished appraising him before answering in the coldest voice she could assemble, "Who wants to know? And would you please step back, my horse is still excited and jumpy from running, I would hate to see you stepped on."

She touched Rap's side lightly with one spur as she spoke, sending him dancing toward the stranger who quickly stepped back to avoid the horse's flying hooves.

Rap wouldn't get excited if someone set firecrackers off under him, Joey thought, she cued him.

"Sorry, I didn't mean to startle him, he's a beautiful animal."

You don't sound very sorry, Sandi and Joey were both thinking.

"Perhaps we could speak alone for a few moments, it's really very important."

I'll bet it is, she thought before replying, "You have quite an approach. What's so important?" As if I didn't know, she added to herself.

"It's a rather delicate matter, but I'm sure you'll understand if you'll only give me a few moments of your time."

33

Well, what can he possibly do to me here with all these people around? Better here than a few other places I can think of, she decided silently. "All right, I suppose I can spare you a few moments. Joey would you excuse us? Just let me put my horse up and we can talk," she added to the stranger as she proceeded to her rig a short distance away.

Joey stared after her completely dumbfounded, Sandi obviously didn't like the guy, yet she had willingly gone off with him. He sat on his horse contemplating the situation and attempting to decipher Sandi's strange actions until a vaguely familiar voice brought him out of his reverie.

"Joey, hey old buddy, how are ya?"

"Steve, I don't believe it, what the hell are you doing here?" He exclaimed.

"It's a long story, but if you've got a minute I'll see if I can condense it." Steven Hoyt answered soberly.

"I take it that this is not a pleasure visit"

"You take it correctly, although it is good to see you, how long has it been now, three, four years?" Steve asked.

"Three years and ten months since I left the high-pressure world of government espionage to break my bones fighting dumb horses and bulls." Joey replied with a grin.

"How would you like to help us out on a little project? Give ya a chance to get shot at instead of stomped on.

"Ah well, might add a little spice to my life, lay it out, I'll see what I can do."

Sandi had ridden to the far side of her rig before dismounting and tying Rap to a hitching ring on the side of it. "All right, she said turning to the cold eyed stranger, "what can...," her voice faded when she found herself looking down the business end of a pistol.

No, she thought, not twice in one day, enough is enough!

"I'm not a very patient man, beautiful, so I suggest you do your best to cooperate. Unless of course, you'd like your pretty face rearranged. Where's the list?"

I've got to stall him, Sandi was thinking as she spoke, "I don't... don't know what you're talking about."

"Don't play dumb with me honey, that might have worked with that chick this morning, but it doesn't cut it with me. You were the first to get to the guy, he had it when I hit him, and he didn't have it when he was searched. That leaves you looking like the culprit in my book. Now be a nice little girl and give it to me so I don't have to get rough."

Damn, I wish his powers of deduction weren't so blasted accurate, somehow I've got to convince him that I don't have it, Sandi said to herself. "Look mister, whoever you are, I don't know, or for that matter care to know, anything about any damn list. That man did not, I repeat, did not give me any list. He was all but dead when I got to him. Search me, search my rig, and then do me a favor, get the hell out of here before I scream the place down and turn you over to the cops."

She was bluffing of course, and it was a long shot that he would believe her. She knew that long before help could arrive, he could have shot and killed her and been long gone. Why did I think I'd be safe here?" Sandi asked herself, looking around she noticed there wasn't a soul in sight.

"Well now that was a real pretty speech, you want to try again, this time with the truth? Oh, by the way, I've already searched your bus and didn't find it, that only leaves you to search," he said with a smug grin.

Oh Lordy, what am I supposed to do now? Is that envelope really worth all this? She asked herself.

"I think you and I should go for a little ride in my car, what do you say?" he inquired.

"I say go to Hell! Right off hand, I can't think of one good reason why I should go anywhere with you."

"How about if I take this here gun and blow a hole in that there horse's head if you don't? Is that a good enough reason to go with me?"

He had guessed her fatal weakness; there was no way that she could let anything happen to her horse. "All right, I'll go with you, but after I put my horse away.

"He'll survive, come on, if you're lucky so will you.

"No, I said I'd go with you, after, and I meant it. Just remember, if I do have your precious list, you'll never find it if you kill me, or my horse."

And neither will anyone else, she thought, I've got to find a way to escape this guy, if I stall long enough maybe, just maybe I'll find a way.

"Okay, do your thing, just remember, no funny stuff, you try anything and I waste you on the spot, list or no list, understand?"

"I understand," she answered dryly as she started to unsaddle Rap, very meticulously undoing all the buckles and putting everything away in the side compartments of the rig. The rear of the bus had been converted into a stall for Rap, with a ramp out the back where the emergency exit had been. She slowly untied Rap and led him around to the rear of the bus to load him when she heard Joey call out to her.

"Sandi, are you all right?" he asked as he approached.

"Fine," she called back, wondering what it felt like to be shot in the back, she was sure the stranger would pull the trigger any moment now.

"What'd that guy want?" he asked as he neared her.

"Joey, listen, I'm going for a drive with him, will you keep an eye on things here for me?"

"You're going for a drive, but not with him my love."

"Joey!" Sandi interrupted, she was bordering on hysteria now, thinking she would be shot any second. "Would you get out of here, I mean it, leave!"

"Sandi, hey it's all right," Joey was close enough to take her by the shoulders and shake her gently now. "Listen to me, he's gone. You're safe; nobody's going to hurt you now." He went on talking but Sandi didn't hear, for the first time in her life she had fainted.

CHAPTER FIVE

When Sandi came to a short while later she was lying on her own bed, she opened her eyes to find herself looking straight into the most fascinating pair of blue eyes she could ever remember. The rest of the man who went with them wasn't bad either, she noted, her mind still more than a little muddled. His dark hair was cut short and combed back away from his face, accentuating his finely chiseled features, hauntingly familiar features.

"Hi there, you ready to join the land of the living again?" the owner of the eyes asked.

Thoughts of the circumstances directly before everything went black came flooding back into her consciousness. "Where's Joey....is he all right my horse.... the guy said held shoot him.....is he all right what happened...who are you?" She fired out the questions with the rapidity of a machine gun, giving him absolutely no time in between to answer-as she struggled to sit up.

"Outside, fine, fine, you fainted and I'm Steven Hoyt. Whew, I think I kept it all straight. Do you always ask so many questions at once?" He queried, pushing her gently back down.

"What happened to the guy with the gun? I remember Joey saying something about him leaving, and then every; good grief, what happened in here?" Sandi had glanced around the interior of the bus as she spoke and saw that everything was in massive turmoil, with the contents of all the cupboards and closets turned out onto the floor, along with the stuffing from miscellaneous cushions and pillows. "Bubbles, where's my dog?" she demanded, again trying unsuccessfully to sit up while Steve tried to calm her. She seemed to remember the stranger saying something about searching her camper, but the meaning hadn't penetrated at the time.

"She's fine, just calm down, Joey's with her right now, everything is under control, and she was only drugged."

"Calm down? You can't be serious, with everything that's happened to me today, you expect me to calm down?" Her voice was several octaves higher than normal by the time she had finished and unshed tears burned her eyes. The fact that he would probably have no way of knowing about everything that had happened to her never even occurred to her right then.

"Listen to me," he shook her shoulders gently, look you're totally exhausted, and, on the verge of hysteria, not that you don't have just cause, but the fact remains, you're not thinking clearly at the moment. If you want answers, I'll be happy to give them to you, if, you will lie still, and quit with the jack-in-the-box routine."

Sandi relaxed back onto her pillow and nodded her head in assent. "I don't see that I have much choice in the matter, who are you to be here telling me what to do anyway?" At the moment she was willing to do almost anything to get him to back away from her, his touch she found too disturbing by far, not unpleasantly disturbing, she realized, in fact far from it.

"I'm an old friend of Joey's, and as I believe I've already said, my name is Steve Hoyt, though I doubt that you were paying a lot of attention at the time." There was a teasing note in his voice and devil's of laughter danced in his eyes, but Sandi was too discomfited right then to notice.

The dying man's words flashed like a neon sign in Sandi's mind, 'Steven Hoyt, Congressman'. I couldn't be so lucky, she thought, not after the way things have been going today. "You wouldn't by any chance be Steven Hoyt, the Congressman, would you?" She asked guardedly while racking her mind to remember if she had ever seen him or a picture of him anywhere.

"One and the same, at your service Ma'am."

"Of course you are," she knew now why his face had seemed familiar to her, "I remember seeing a picture of you somewhere, I'm afraid it wasn't very flattering, it definitely did not do justice to those gorgeous blue eyes of yours, but then newspaper pictures rarely do." Sandi found herself rambling, saying things that she could never imagine herself saying to any man, much less this self-assured image of a Greek God sitting before her. She stopped speaking suddenly, a rosy blush spread quickly up her cheeks.

Could she possibly know something, Steve asked himself hopefully. He tried to think of something to say to her that would put her more at ease but found himself almost mesmerized into silence by her, she looked so small and helpless lying there. He realized that his thoughts were ridiculously far from the subject at hand, but there was no denying their existence.

They stared at one another for a moment in silence before starting to speak simultaneously, they both stopped at once, indicating the other should continue. The results reminded Sandi of a routine in a slapstick comedy she had seen years before, she had to practically bite her tongue to keep from laughing out loud. Why she should feel so lighthearted and happy all of a sudden didn't bear looking into right then, she knew all ready that it wasn't just because she could get the list off her hands.

"You first."

"No, by all means, please continue," Steve acquiesced.

"No, no, it's all right, you go ahead."

"Ladies first."

"Oh all right," Sandi finally took the bull by the horns. "I just didn't think I could be so lucky. Having you come to me, I mean, I thought I was going to have to go to Washington to find you."

Steve looked puzzled; it was rapidly becoming obvious that she really did know something. Maybe she had the list, or at least knew something of its whereabouts.

But no, that would be too much to hope for, it would be too easy.

"I suppose I should begin at the beginning..." she hesitated.

"It might be easier, although I suppose I could save some time by asking a few questions, I'd rather hear the whole story... if you don't mind that is."

"Of course not, I suppose you know about the accident, only I guess it really wasn't an accident, this morning."

Had it really only been that morning, it seemed more like days ago. Steve proved to be an excellent listener, interrupting only to clarify details.

"Your turn," Sandi told him when she had finally finished. "Why are you here, you couldn't have known that I had the envelope? Could you?"

"Known, no, I think hoped would be a better description. But that wasn't the whole reason, we, meaning the United States government, sent me to try to talk you into allowing us to protect you. I suppose I put that rather badly. But you see this situation is rather delicate, and about as explosive as a case of nitro. The people on the other side have absolutely no compunction about killing to get their way. Or to be even more specific, if someone gets in their way, inadvertently you have, you see, they are looking for the list too. "And they may try to get me to give it to them." Sandi finished for him. "They have all ready you know, that guy, the one I thought was going to shoot me, he wanted the list. From what he said he was the one who ran the man down this morning. You never answered my question."

"Which one?"

"What happened to him, the guy with the gun, did you catch him?"

Steve shook his head, "I'm afraid not, he slipped off as soon as he saw us. He'd let you get too far away to grab you, that's what we were most afraid of, if he'd taken you hostage, we'd have played hell getting you away from him. I didn't think he would just kill you, not yet anyway, not until he has located the list."

"Well, now that you're here I can give the list to you and be on my merry way." Somehow that thought didn't bring the joy and relief it should have.

"It's not quite that easy, you see when we were checking you out," he held up a hand when she started to protest, her eyes flashing with anger. "We had to Babe, I'm sorry, but this is much too vital not to have. We had to know who you were, and anything any computer in the country could tell us. You have a photographic memory don't you?"

"Some people call it that, there are more technical terms, but basically it amounts to an excellent memory, especially if I see whatever it is I want to remember."

"Such as the list?"

"Yes," she answered simply.

"You did look at it didn't you?"

"I thought it would be better, at least then I'd be able to reconstruct it if anything should happen to it. I didn't understand any of it though; it was in some sort of code I think." She added hastily.

"I understand, but you must understand that if they find out about your memory they'll try to get you to tell them what it said."

"So what happens now? Do you hide me away in some sleazy motel under another name, with several bodyguards?"

"That's one way, but I have another. It's not all worked out yet so I'd rather not tell you what it is." He looked her straight in the eye. "Will you trust me; just do as I say, no questions just yet, on my plan at any rate?"

Right then Sandi realized she would probably trust him if he told her to jump off a cliff, you can fly! It was frightening, she hardly knew the man. "Yes... Yes I'll trust you," she heard herself say while a part of her mind screamed out in protest, but it was only a small part, apparently the only-part that controlled her common sense.

"Good girl, I knew I could count on you," he looked around the bus. "Quite a mess your friend left behind."

"I needed to do some spring cleaning; I just hadn't planned on starting with all the cupboards at once." She had picked up on his desire to change the subject. "Is it all right if I sit up now?" My heads stopped spinning…"

"Sure, just be careful, you scared the hell out of Joey, he thought you'd been hurt. I finally had to send him out with your dog just to get him out of the way to find out if you really were hurt."

Sandi smiled at the picture he had presented, she could just imagine it.

"If you'll just sit still and tell me where things go I'll try to straighten up for you," he offered.

She looked at him trying to picture him doing housework but failed miserably, in fact, the whole business suddenly struck her as being rather funny. Here was one of the most incredibly handsome and masculine men she had ever met looking her straight in the eye and offering to clean up her rig. After all she had been through since dawn it somehow didn't fit into the context of her day and she started to giggle.

"What's the joke?" Steve asked, seriously, not seeing one iota of humor in their circumstances.

"This... Sandi managed to get out between giggles, waving her hand to indicate the interior of the rig, "and you.... offering to play maid." And with that she broke into gales of laughter. It must have been infectious, for Steve started to laugh too.

"Behold the great Congressman Hoyt, complete with apron..." Sandi contrived.

"Now wait a minute," Steve managed, "I never said I was going to make a career of it, or that I'd be very adept at it. But I think I can manage a few simple tasks without making a complete fool of myself."

49

It was this jovial scene that Joey walked in on, after leaving in a state of anxiety over Sandi; he wasn't too sure how to take this complete reversal of her mood. I guess it's nothing new, I've been having trouble figuring her out all day, he thought.

"Anyone going to fill me in on the joke?" He asked when they had calmed down a little.

"Steve..." Sandi started to explain.

"Don't you dare say one word young woman, or Steve threatened.

"Yes Mr. Hoyt," Sandi interrupted, "you'll what, believe me, I've been threatened so many times today I doubt that one more will make a great deal of difference."

Bubbles, a medium sized, Heinz 57 variety of dog, was lying rather groggily in Joey's arms. When she heard Sandi's voice she proceeded to struggle fiercely for her freedom, knocking him slightly off balance in the process. When he attempted to recover he tripped over part of the mess on the floor and wound up sprawled in the middle of all the chaos with a very upset Bubbles on top. The whole scene sent them all off with gales of laughter, temporarily forgetting their troubles.

CHAPTER SIX

Sandi drove Steve to a nearby airfield where the helicopter he had arrived in was waiting for him, while Joey followed behind in his pickup. "Are you sure you're up to driving all the way to Washington tonight Sandi, you know we can do this a different way if you aren't?" Steve asked her as she braked to a stop.

"I can make it, Steve, don't worry about me. This isn't the first time I've gone without sleep and it probably won't be the last. You two think it's the safest way, so that's the way we'll do it. If I start to get drowsy I'll turn up the radio, or talk to Joey on the CB," she reassured him.

"All right, but be careful, we can change plans if we have to. I don't want you taking any unnecessary risks; you're in enough danger as it is." Steve said as he got out. For some unknown reason, he felt a strange reluctance to leave her, it wasn't just that she was in jeopardy, he realized, there was more to it than that. He wanted to be near her. It was a strange new feeling that he wasn't sure he wanted to delve into too deeply at the moment.

Sandi watched Steve jog across the tarmac to the waiting helicopter before glancing at her watch. "Ten o'clock," she muttered, "It must be about thirty-six hours now since I've slept unless I count that few minute nap when I passed out. Another four to five hours and I should resemble a walking zombie."

A light misty rain began to fall as she drove out onto the highway. Mother Nature must be in the same mood I'm in, she thought, just what we need right now, a good storm. With that, it did begin to rain harder.

After a rather lengthy discussion, mostly between Steve and Joey, final plans for their journey to Washington had been settled on. Sandi and Joey were to drive in their own vehicles, caravan style, while Steve watched from a helicopter for any interference. He would be able to see if they were being followed or if anyone tried to stop them along the way in which case he would signal two agents who were driving a short distance ahead of them in an unmarked car. Hopefully, anyone watching would think that Steve was carrying the list, and that there wasn't much they could do to him while he was in the air. Sandi had tried to give the list to him, but he had decided that her hiding place was better than any he could come up with, for her to just leave it there.

Sandi had learned that the two men had known each other since boyhood, had served as Navy Seals together, and had then worked as undercover agents for the government until a few years before. At that time Steve had run for and was elected to the Senate and Joey had bought a ranch in Arizona. Supposedly the ranch hadn't done too well so he had started following the rodeo circuit.

As she drove her thoughts drifted back over the last few hours since he had awakened to Steve's brilliant blue eyes staring down at her. She thought of his care and concern for her safety, of his consideration for her wishes, the way he had tried to calm her fears. She realized that so long as he was near her she felt quite safe and almost cherished. Joey had been a good friend for a long time now, he even claimed to love her, but for some unexplainable reason Steve was different. It had been a very long time since she had felt so drawn to a man, both physically and emotionally, and that was a very disturbing thought.

Without desiring it, her thoughts slowly slipped back to other times when she had loved and thought herself to be, only to find that she had been cruelly deceived. Sandi was only eighteen when she married Peter, and he had been her husband for only a few hours, when overhearing a phone conversation, she learned that he was only interested in her grandfather's money. It seemed he had gambled himself into debt and felt that Sandi's grandfather would pay off his debts to protect her from embarrassment. Of course, she wasn't supposed to have discovered this quite the way she had, nor had he allowed for Sandi's reaction to the news. After a terrible row in the suite at their hotel in Hawaii where they were to have spent their honeymoon, she had simply walked out, and gone home.

Her parents had been horrified, Peter was from such a fine upstanding family, and Sandi should have done something to save their marriage. She had always known that social standing was important to her parents, but until then she had never known that it meant quite so much. Her grandfather had finally stepped in, simply stating that he would take care of everything, and packed her off to some quiet resort in the San Bernardino Mountains to recover from the shock. Many people believed she had divorced Peter, while in fact, the marriage had been annulled. How the rumor got started she never knew although she had her suspicions, but somehow it didn't seem worth the bother to set the record straight, she much preferred to forget the whole episode.

Four years later Alan entered her life and took it by storm. They met at a small dinner party and were married two short weeks later. For one year she had been blissfully happy, ignorant bliss she soon discovered. Alan was often away driving in races, she had found that it upset her too much to watch, so she usually waited at home in a small house Alan had purchased near her grandfather's California ranch. During his frequent absences, she could usually be found training the young horses and doing odd jobs on the ranch which helped her control her loneliness and anxiety.

Alan was in Germany for the Nuremberg race on their first anniversary, he had promised they would celebrate when he returned. She decided at the last minute to fly over so they could be together for their 'special day'.

It never occurred to her that he might not want her presence, so she didn't call and tell him of her arrival, deciding to go straight to his hotel and surprise him. It turned out that she was the one surprised however, when she arrived to find him in the arms of his best friend's wife. Afterward, she could never remember exactly what was said, only that there had been an appalling quarrel, during which he had accused her of being childish and immature. Then he had walked out taking his companion with him. That was the last time she had seen him alive, the next day he was killed when his car was hit and it burst into flames.

The entire experience had left her lost and confused, had Alan been right, was she childish and immature, living in a fairy tale world, and unable to face the realities of life? It was a question she had asked herself thousands of times since that fateful day in Germany. Somehow she would have to find the answer before she could love again.

Joey watched the windshield wipers rhythmically swishing the rain away leaving him a clearer view of the highway. Not unlike the incidents of the past few hours clearing his mind, letting him look into the past again. He had successfully blocked the memory of Barbara and their last argument just before he had quit the agency from his mind for almost three years now. He realized now that even though he had refused to even think about her, he had never stopped loving her. That even though he cared a great deal for Sandi, it was really Barbara that held the key to his heart, and it appeared she always would. He had wanted her to quit the agency and be his wife, finding that he couldn't work and worry about her at the same time. But Barbara loved her work and didn't want to quit, neither of them would compromise. As a last resort Joey had bought the ranch, he had hoped to persuade her to quit the agency and go with him, but she had refused. But now he was coming back, would he see her he wondered? Was she one of the agents in the car ahead? Maybe, if he tried, he could learn to live the way she wanted. Unless she had found someone else, perhaps she was now married. The thought of her with someone else left him shaken. How could I have been so stupid, how could I have just let her go? He asked himself.

CHAPTER SEVEN

It was several seconds after she awoke before Sandi realized where she was. She sat up slowly in the big four-poster bed blinking her eyes and trying to clear the fog that heavy sleep had left in her mind. Leaning back on one elbow she looked around, studying the room she was in. It was beautifully decorated in pale to royal blues and write, the furniture was French Provincial, and obviously very old, probably antique, she thought, but it was just as obvious that it had received loving care down through the years. Though not pretentiously, wealth was indicated throughout the entire room.

Slowly as her mind began to function, the memory of their early morning arrival at Steve's home in Georgetown, a residential district of Washington DC, came back to her. Steve had decided that so long as the list was safe, it was not urgent that it be delivered right then, in the middle of the night. It could just as easily be taken to the agency after they had all received some much-needed rest, especially Sandi. She couldn't have agreed with him more, she had been rapidly working on two days without sleep and even for a dedicated insomniac that was pushing it.

The last thing she felt up to right then was answering another gross of questions about how the list came to be in her possession.

Unfortunately, her memory of their arrival consisted mainly of disconnected scenes. She only vaguely recalled Steve insisting that she sleep in one of his guest rooms rather than trying to stumble through the chaotic mess still on the floor of her bus, and there was something about him taking care of her animals too. They had arrived at a large estate, or at least it had seemed so, and there had been several people milling about, who they were, she didn't know, and at the time she hadn't really cared. Steve had run around barking out orders to everyone, everyone that is except herself, she seemed to recall. It wouldn't have mattered if he had barked at me too, she thought, I was too tired to have cared if I had even heard him. Even now in the light of day her mind shied clear of examining whether or not his solicitous manner toward herself was real or imaginative wishful thinking, or what his motive was if it really did exist.

Recalling the importance of the list served to jog her out of her daydreams and into action. "Whoops," she said aloud when throwing back the sheets she realized that she was attired in only her birthday suit. First things first, where the hell are my clothes? I don't even remember taking them off, she thought. She flushed as her thoughts went through A list of possible interpretations of their disappearance, at the top of which, who removed them from her body?

She finally found them, freshly cleaned and pressed, hanging in a large walk-in closet leading off of the dressing room, opposite a private bath.

Sandi had barely finished dressing after taking a quick shower when a light tap on the door heralded the entrance of a rather plump elderly woman. "I thought I heard you moving about, I'm Sarah, Mr. Steve's housekeeper," She said, smiling at Sandi, "Mr. Steve said that you were not to be disturbed for any reason short of the house burning down." Sarah added as she bustled over to the windows and proceeded to open the shades, letting in abundantly more of the bright spring sunlight than was already seeping through.

"I'm Sandi, did you do my clothes? I certainly appreciate it, but I had more in my bus." She really wanted to ask how they had come to be off of her, but wasn't all that sure that she wanted to hear the answer. "Oh, they weren't any bother, Mr. Steve, said that he wasn't sure what condition your others were in. He told me about your bus being broken into my dear." She shook her head sadly, "I don't know what this world is coming to with all this vandalism going on. Now, I'll bet you'd like some breakfast, wouldn't you?"

"I'd love some," Sandi answered, acknowledging her grumbling stomach for the first time, "it seems like I haven't eaten in days."

"Considering that you slept all day yesterday, it..."

"I what? What day is this?" Sandi asked incredulously.

"Why it's Tuesday, dear." Sarah answered.

"Tuesday! I had no idea, I knew that I felt awfully rested for only a few hours sleep, but I can't believe I slept for that long." Steve must be having fits.

"Now don't you fret, Mr. Steve isn't even here. He said to tell you that he would be back in a few hours if you woke while he was out. You're to have a nice breakfast and if you feel like it, I'll show you around after that. He thought you might like to go down to the stables and check on your horse and dog. I saw your horse yesterday; my he's a pretty thing isn't he."

"What...oh, yes... thank you," Sandi managed brokenly. She couldn't understand why Steve had let her sleep so long, she had never really gotten around to telling him exactly where the list was, only that she had hidden it in some tack. Short of tearing every piece of her horse's tack completely apart she doubted if he would have found it, so he probably had not delivered the list yet, it just didn't make sense.

After having a large delicious breakfast, served to her outside in the warm sunshine on a terrace over looking a gorgeous garden at the side of the house, of scrambled eggs, bacon, toast and coffee that no one could say she had not done justice to, Sandi went in search of her animals. Her impression that Steve's home was on a large estate had not been wrong, it probably consisted of several acres of exquisitely landscaped land. The stable area, which Sarah had directed her to, was a hundred or so yards behind the house in amongst several very large and beautiful old oak trees. Rap and Bubbles greetings were exuberant, to say the least, leaving her no doubt that they had missed her though they appeared to have been very well cared for in her absence. After spending some minutes with them she returned to the house for Sarah's promised tour, history fascinated her, so a tour and old homes had always fascinated her, so a tour of a colonial mansion was not something to be passed up. Of course, knowing, and being more interested than she was willing to admit even to herself in the owner of such a place gave her additional incentive.

Sarah, she learned, had been Steve's governess and had stayed employed by the family in one capacity or another ever since. Sandi had raised her eyebrows at that tidbit of knowledge. Though she said nothing it had come as rather a shock to learn that Steve had been born more or less of the silver-spoon-in-the-mouth group, having met several in her life he had not struck her as the type, in fact far from it. It wasn't as though she had expected him to have come from a poor family, she realized after some thought, he just didn't fit into any particular classification, he was in a group all his own, and all alone.

There wasn't any doubt that Sarah was as proud as any mother could be of her own son when it came to Steve, telling Sandi about him as a child and showing her pictures of him growing up.

The house was of the Georgian era, built some time in the 1750's by one of Steve's distant ancestors. It had passed out of the family's possession for three or four generations only to be purchased by a great-great uncle of his. Steve had inherited it from his grandfather several years before and had set about restoring it to its original splendor. As far as Sandi was concerned he had done a magnificent job of it.

Sarah chatted incessantly during the entire tour about Steve and the family she had been employed by for so many years. In fact, the only thing Sandi found her to be reticent about was the portrait of a very beautiful woman and Steve in the study. She longed to ask who the woman was but did not want to appear overtly curious.

While Sarah was in charge of the house staff, her husband, Bill, supervised the maintenance of the gorgeous gardens and spacious lawns surrounding the colonnaded mansion. When Sarah had finished taking Sandi around the interior, Bill showed her the park like-grounds around it, pointing out the different species of flora imported from all parts of the world. Indicating the newly formed buds that marked the first signs of spring, he assured her that in a few weeks the gardens would be a riot of colors.

Again and again she was told that "Mr. Steve", as he was called by the entire staff, wanted her to make herself at home. If she wished to swim, there was a lovely heated pool, if she wished to ride her horse, there was an exercise ring, and if she wished to play tennis, someone on the staff would accommodate her. The only reminders that she was not at some fancy resort on vacation were the several men unobtrusively patrolling the grounds and at the gates, men whom she had been told were there for her protection.

Steve still had not shown up by the time Sarah and Bill had finished taking her around so she decided to spend some time cleaning and straightening away the confused mass of her belongings on the floor of the bus. She had put off the project as long as her conscience would allow her to. Sarah offered to help, but Sandi politely turned her down, explaining that it wouldn't take her all that long. She needed the time alone to sort out her thoughts, though she didn't tell Sarah that, everything was happening so fast, not the least of which was the unexplainable interest in her host, who was undoubtedly in love with the beautiful woman in the portrait. She simply could not allow herself to fall for a man that was in love with someone else; that could and would only lead to certain heartache. There ought to be a law against a man being as attractive as he is, she thought, angrily slamming the door of her rig, her task accomplished.

I guess I should let Rap out of his stall to run for awhile, Steve's still not here.

A few minutes later Sandi watched as Rap and Bubbles chased each other around the paddock in play. She was unaware that the tall, blue-eyed man so much in her thoughts the last few hours had arrived and was now gazing wonderingly at her.

Steve leaned negligently against a large magnolia tree watching the sunlight play down on Sandi's shinny brown curls. What makes her so damn special? He asked himself. Why is it that every time I'm near her I have this urge to take her in my arms? I've met some of the most beautiful women in the world and not felt one tenth of the attraction for them that I feel for her. It would be just my luck to fall for a buddy's girl. Joey always could pick 'em. Damn it to hell, how am I going to keep my hands off her if she agrees to our plan? He shrugged resolutely, I guess I'll just have to wait and see what happens, she will probably tell us to go to hell. With that he walked down the path to where Sandi was leaning on the fence of the exercise ring.

"They seem to be enjoying themselves." Steve spoke softly from behind her causing her to spin around in surprise, "I didn't mean to startle you. How are you feeling?"

"Guilty, if you must know, why didn't you wake me?"

Because you were worn out, the list was safe, thanks to you, so I decided that one day more or less wasn't going to matter that much."

"Are you sure?" I couldn't believe it when Sarah told me that it was Tuesday. I've never slept like that before in my life.

"Have you ever been through an experience like this before?" he asked.

"Well, no... but still..."

"Still nothing! Quit letting it bother you," he ordered harshly, "There's someone in my study that would like to talk to you, if you feel up to it." His voice softened as soon as he saw her stricken look from his tone of voice.

"Of course, is it about the list? Do you want me to get it?"

"Here we go again," he laughed, then explained when she looked puzzled, "Do you ever ask just one question at a time?"

67

"Sorry, I guess it's a bad habit," she apologized, looking sheepish.

"No, don't apologize, I was only teasing, besides it keeps me on my toes keeping the answers straight. Incidentally, yes and yes are the answers to the last two. Shall we go?" he asked, "Your horse will be fine where he is for awhile, Bill will put him away later."

"Okay," She answered, "Where's Joey? I haven't seen him, isn't he staying here too?" She put her hand up to her mouth, "Oh no, I just did it again didn't I?" But because Steve laughed and seemed to think it was funny she didn't feel all that embarrassed.

Steve was laughing in spite of himself, as much as her bringing Joey's name into the conversation bothered him, he still found her adorable, much to adorable to be very upset with. "He's taking care of some business, yes and yes," he replied good-naturedly.

"Now I can understand why that guy couldn't find this thing," Steve said after they had spent several minutes retrieving the envelope. "A very unique, but effective, hiding place. How'd you come up with it?"

"Accident, I racked my brains all day for a place, then when I was getting ready to saddle Rap for the rodeo I remembered the sheep-skin was pulling away there on the skirt of the saddle. I started to just glue it back when I thought what a good place it would be to hide the envelope. As it turned out, while that guy was searching my rig for it, I was sitting on it."

"Very ingenious," he commented as he opened the door of his study then stepped back allowing her to enter first.

A short, stocky man in his fifties was standing by the window; he turned and greeted them when they entered. "So this is our reluctant courier. Steve and Joey have both been singing your praises to me. Please, sit down, I'm dying to hear how you acquired the thankless job of delivering the list."

"Sandi, meet Wayne Groiter, Wayne, Sandra Stanford." Steve introduced them as they all sat down. "You'll never believe where she hid the list Wayne. We could have turned that bus upside down and inside out and never found it."

"I'm just glad that I don't have to worry about it anymore." Sandi said thankfully, "I think if I'd known what I was getting myself into when I ran out to that poor man, I would have had second thoughts! But it's over now, the list is safely delivered and I've survived."

"So far, you've survived," Steve stated bluntly.

"Sandi, I realize that you stumbled into this unaware of what you were g6tting into. At the risk of upsetting you further I have to explain that for the next several weeks you are going to be in very grave danger." Wayne stated quietly.

"Several weeks?" Sandi replied in disbelief, "Steve told me that it would be until things were settled, I guess I just assumed that he meant a few days, but several weeks?"

"I'm sorry Sandi, but I'm afraid it can't be helped, we'll do everything in our power to ensure your safety and comfort. In fact we've come up with a plan I hope will meet with your approval, although I've been forewarned that it probably won't. But first, I'd like to hear how you managed to get Nash to give you this list." Wayne said as he opened the envelope Steve had handed him and gave it a cursory glance.

"He just handed it to me; I didn't even know what it was. He said 'Take this, protect it with your life, must get to Steven Hoyt, no one else, could mean war, please,' then I had trouble understanding him, but I think he said, 'Congressman, Washington, tell him to look', that was it, I couldn't make out the rest. I don't know what I was supposed to tell Steve to look at or for."

"I don't get it Steve, why you, why not me, or the President, and why give it to a stranger when he knew that Barbara was his contact? It just doesn't make sense."

"I don't know Wayne, we may never know, but at least we have it now. I just wish I knew what I was supposed to look for….or at."

"Sandi, why didn't you ask for Barbara's help when she told you who she was?" Wayne inquired.

"Nash said 'no one else', how was I supposed to know she was really who she said she was? For all I knew the truck driver may have been the good guy. I really didn't know what to do, I almost asked the police for help. I had just watched a man get murdered for something I was carrying around, if I did wrong I'm sorry, but to say I was slightly upset at the time would be the understatement of the century."

"Hey, calm down, you didn't do a thing wrong." Steve interrupted her. "We're just trying to figure out why Nash gave you the list, and why he said to give it to me and 'no one else'."

"Tell you what, when you figure it out, let me know, I just did what I was told."

"And you did a fantastic job, I'm sorry; I didn't mean to insinuate that you had done anything wrong when I asked that question." Wayne apologized, "Giving it to Barbara would have been a natural reaction for most people, believe me, there isn't any way for us to thank you enough for what you did."

"I'm sorry too; I guess it still gets to me, the way he died and all."

"Let's tell her our plan, Steve, then if you and Joey are right, she'll really be ready to tell us all to go to, permanently. But it ought to take her mind off Nash."

"Is it really that bad?" she asked, taking Wayne's hint for a change of subject gratefully. The other subject still upset her entirely too much. "I've been told that I'm rather unpredictable, so maybe I'll like your plan."

"I doubt it." Steve replied dryly.

"Would I be wrong in thinking that you're not particularly fond of it yourself, Steve?" She asked.

"I never said that, I just don't happen to think that you're going to like it. Actually it was mostly my idea."

"I see, well, one of you tell me what it is, so we can get the suspense over with."

"You want to tell her Steve or shall I?"

"Oh, you tell her, I'll just sit back and watch the sparks fly."

"Thanks, remind me that I owe you one! Okay, Sandi, first of all, will you promise to hear me out, before you tell us off?"

"I wish you'd just tell me and get it over with."

"All right, now understand that we had to find a place for you to stay that number one, we could secure against intruders. Number-two, where you could be relatively comfortable, and number three, where you could keep your horse and dog. I was informed that you are rather attached to those two and refused to leave them at the fair grounds. So....we decided the best place would be right here at Steve's."

"I don't understand, other than the fact that Steve gets dumped with an uninvited guest, I don't mind."

"You're not uninvited and he isn't finished yet." Steve retorted quietly.

"You see Sandi; you won't exactly be a guest. Steve is an unmarried senator, and even in this day and age, with free love and all that sort of thing, a man in his position doesn't live with an unmarried woman, unless held like to kiss his career good-bye."

Somehow she knew what he was going to say but was absolutely powerless to stop him.

"Steve is a very popular person in more ways than one," Wayne continued, "In Washington, there are something like four or five girls to every man. Steve's name is quite often in the social column of the newspaper, and, he isn't without enemies..."

Get to the point Wayne." Steve interrupted impatiently, "And quit making me out to be some sort of Don Juan."

"I just wanted Sandi to understand the basis .of our decision. We want you and Steve to be married; now it's only temporary, just until we are sure you are completely out of danger."

There was a stunned silence while Sandi slowly digested this last turn of events. Even though she had seen it coming, it was still something of a shock to hear it actually being put into words. Gradually a smile touched her lips. "Behold me, an average American girl, who in the process of being a Good Samaritan, winds up carrying top secret government papers. And, with her life in perilous danger, she marries a senator that she has never met before in her life! Do you know that I would be declared certifiably insane if I told anyone about this? They would never believe me, I'm here, and I don't believe it."

"But you'll do it?' Wayne prompted.

"Correct me if I'm wrong, but I don't recall you giving me any other alternatives." She turned to Steve, "You really think this is the best way to go Steve?"

"I think it will serve the purpose," he answered noncommittally.

"Which is a polite way of saying I shouldn't question your ideas."

"Who knows what's best Sandi?" he asked despondently, "I don't have a crystal ball, I don't know the future, but I'm willing to try this if you are."

"Well, I guess, I certainly don't want to be responsible for ruining your career. And I certainly don't want to try handling things on my own, my adrenal glands have worked enough over time lately, fear has a funny way of causing that," she responded while thinking, but what about the girl in the portrait? Where does she fit in?

"Good, then it's all settled," Wayne broke in before she could change her mind. "You'll be married here, this afternoon."

"This afternoon? I've heard of short engagements, but this is ridiculous... but this is ridiculous... What about blood tests, don't we need a license?" She asked; her voice slightly higher than normal.

"Everything will be taken care of. Some things can be speeded up if you know how," Wayne answered.

"No kidding!" Was the only response she could think of.

CHAPTER EIGHT

Wayne's announcement of their impending wedding left Sandi in a state of shock, and she found herself unable to follow much of the subsequent conversation. Questions kept popping unbidden into her mind, like how was she going to hide her unexplainable attraction to Steve from him over the next several weeks? Who was the girl in the portrait hanging on the wall directly behind her? Would any man keep a picture like that around if he wasn't in love with her, and how was this girl going to react to the news of their marriage? None of these questions made the immediate future look particularly promising and left Sandi in an ill-tempered frame of mind. Wayne was taking his leave, vowing to return later for the ceremony when she finally surfaced from her depressing thoughts.

"I believe lunch will be ready," Steve said, closing the beautiful, solid oak front door behind Wayne.

"I'm not very hungry, why don't you go on?" Sandi replied, turning away. She needed some time alone to sort out her jumbled thoughts, but Steve wasn't letting her escape that easily. His hand shot out and she felt a warm thrill streak through her veins as his fingers closed around her arm just above the elbow.

"I know you're feeling slightly disconcerted by all this Sandi," he said as he wrenched her around to face him. "But don't let it get you down. It will all be over with in a few weeks and everything will return to normal."

"You'll have to excuse me if I find that hard to believe," she retorted dryly, trying to ignore what his touch was doing to her senses.

"If it's any consolation, I can think of things more convenient to have happen at this time myself."

She flinched inwardly from the bluntness of his statement, her temper coming to her rescue. "Well, pardon me," she replied sarcastically, "I don't recall being asked if it was convenient for me to risk my neck getting that damn list to you! Has anyone asked me if it's convenient for me to just drop my life and play housewife to a stranger for the next several weeks? Does...

"That's enough!" he interrupted her harshly, "I refuse to stand here and discuss the injustices of life with you. My main concern is your safety for the next few weeks; our getting married appears to be the best way of accomplishing that feat. I was hoping that you wouldn't be quite so adverse to the prospects"

"You refuse! That's royal, I refuse to stand here and be manhandled by you, in other words, let go of my arm. I may have to marry you, but let's get one thing..." That was all she managed to get out before she was roughly jerked against Steve's hard frame and his lips closed over hers, effectively silencing her outburst. Against her will she felt her body respond to his nearness and touch, then just as abruptly as she had found herself in his arms she found herself out of them.

"I'm sorry, I had no right to do that.... but it was the only way I could think of to shut you up."

"I see," Sandi answered quietly, hoping he wouldn't hear the catch in her voice.

"No, I don't think you do. May I suggest that we go for a short walk and I'll try to explain? I had intended to do so over lunch, however," he added with a half grin "your temper is rather volatile and I'd rather not be overheard."

"I'm sorry," she apologized with mixed emotions, not sure whether she was really sorry or not. "I guess I'm a little touchy at the moment."

"Let's forget it, I'm as much to blame as you. Shall we?" he indicated the door that he had just reopened.

Neither said anything more for a few moments as they made their way down the verandah steps and followed a path around the house and into the gardens. Sandi was too busy getting her emotions back on an even keel and sorting out her thoughts to ask any questions. While Steve was berating himself for his own actions, knowing full well that now it would be harder than ever to keep her at arm's length. Each was totally unaware of the other's tormenting thoughts.

"I don't normally act the way I just did," Steve was the first to break the silence. "Do you think we could start our conversation over?"

"And go through all that again?" Sandi made a half-hearted attempt at lightness. "Why don't we just drop it all together? Do you really believe that our getting married is the best way, or are you just saying that for my benefit?"

Steve choose to ignore the first two questions. "Sandi there is one thing that you can believe if nothing else, I would not have suggested it, or for that matter, agreed to it if someone else had, if I didn't think it was the best way to keep you safe. There are certain matters pertaining to this case that you know nothing about, and I don't have the authority to tell you or I would. But be assured your safety and comfort are very important, and I'll do whatever is necessary to provide you with them. Will you believe that?"

She nodded, feeling more than a little ashamed for questioning him. After all, he was marrying her while in love with someone else. If I were his girl I wouldn't be too pleased that he was marrying another girl, even if it was only temporary and for her safety. She must be very special.

"Good, then let me explain a few details of the plan that Wayne didn't cover. In order for this to work, we must make our marriage appear to be quite real, in other words, a marriage based on love. A certain amount of publicity can't be avoided, I'll limit it: as much as I can, but an unexpected union like ours is going to cause some speculation. There are only four people who know the real reason, Wayne, Joey, you, and I, as far as anyone else is concerned we have known each other for some time and managed to keep it quiet. Even the staff in my home can't suspect anything, which is going to require some acting on our part."

"I'm to play the part of the blushing bride?"

"Well, if not blushing, at least happy. Hence my desire to shut you up in there, before we were over-heard by someone. I do want you to understand that I won't make a habit of it, all I ask is that when we are where we can be seen or heard you play the loving wife. If you wish you don't even have to speak to me otherwise."

"I don't think I need to go to that extreme, I'm sorry for getting so upset in there. This situation has me a little off course. It all seems so unreal somehow ' you read in novels about stuff like this, but never dream of it happening in real life, least of all to yourself."

"I understand, just remember, we all want you to live through this, and to do that, you and I must convince everyone that we are happily married."

"I'll do my best," she assured him, while thinking that it shouldn't be too difficult to act like she loved him, she was already half way there. The difficult part was going to be to not act that way when they were alone. But what choice did she have, she had to go along with their plan.

"I was sure we could count on you. Now then, perhaps you would like to phone your family and tell them of our marriage, unless you would rather they read about it in the newspapers tomorrow."

"I suppose I should call my parents and grandfather," adding dryly, "Mother can be relied upon to tell anyone else that needs to know. She will undoubtedly be over the moon about this. Her main goal in life has been to see me marry well, which a Congressman can be described as. I'm assuming that they can't be told the truth either?"

"Sorry, but at the present, no. I will be happy to help you explain the situation to them when the time comes."

"Let's just hope you are a good liar now. My parents will accept what I say without question, but Grandpa is a different kettle of fish all together. I wouldn't put it past him to fly to Washington this afternoon to look you over personally."

"He must think a. lot of *you*."

"We're very close, I think you would take to him, Mother says I'm like him, in too many ways. All I know is that he has picked up the pieces of me after my last two attempts at the game of matrimony. I'm not sure I even want to think about his reaction to this attempt. He may wash his hands of me all together, give me up as a lost cause," she told him sadly.

"It won't be long before you can explain it all to him, Sandi," he reassured her softly, wondering why her unhappiness affected him so much. "Just remember it's for a good cause."

"I'll keep telling myself that," she commented skeptically. "Maybe if I keep it up long enough I'll manage to convince myself. You had better fill me in on what you plan on releasing to the press, it wouldn't look too good if our stories didn't match."

Steve spent the next several minutes telling Sandi of the story that Wayne, Joey and he had come up with. He didn't mention anything about Joey's reaction to this plan and Sandi wondered what it had been. She was sure that Joey could not have been overly pleased about it, he had told her repeatedly that he loved her and had asked her to marry him more than once. She must be in very grave danger indeed for Joey to agree to a plan like this, even if it was only temporary. It was either that or she had finally managed to convince him that she didn't love him in return and he had finally given up.

"Can you think of anything we left out?" Steve's question brought Sandi out of her pondering.

"What...oh... no nothing that I can think of off-hand, I'm sure that you thought of everything," she answered, trying to recall exactly what he had said. I really am going to have to quit letting my mind wander so much, she reflected.

"We may have to do some ad-libbing as we go, but you have the general -idea. I'll try not to get too specific about anything; I think it will be easier that way. We should try to stick close to each other this afternoon, and then we will know what the other has said. The reception is going to be the hardest part."

"The reception? I wasn't aware that we were having one," she looked at him with surprise, what else had she missed, or had he planned without telling her?

"I thought it would look better, only a few very close friends and my grandmother, Wayne will be there of course. Joey won't probably be back yet. My grandmother is the only relative either one of us will have attending, she lives here in town. I've always been close to her, like you and your grandfather. Maybe that's why I can understand your reluctance to tell him. Somehow, people like that are the most difficult to not be completely honest with. But enough of this, time is flying, we need to go eat lunch, then you can make your calls. Sarah needs to be given a little notice that we are entertaining this afternoon and evening."

"You mean that you haven't told her yet? Knowing how most housekeepers were she thought it would be a miracle if Sarah didn't walk out on him without anymore notice than he was giving her.

"And have her say something to you before Wayne and I had a chance to explain things. I can just see your reaction if Sarah had greeted you with that this morning."

"I see your point, I might not have said quite the right things to that." She smiled at the picture it presented.

Immediately after Sarah had served their lunch Steve dropped the news of their wedding on poor unsuspecting Sarah. She had nearly fainted with surprise before it struck her that there were preparations to be made and she bustled off, madly firing out orders to the staff as she went. Apparently Steve knew his housekeeper better than Sandi thought, Sarah hadn't even protested about the lack of preparation time.

As Sandi had predicted her mother and father were elated with the prospect of having a senator for a son-in-law. There were a few touchy moments when Sandi explained that they could not fly out to California to be married, much less attend the reception that her mother wanted to hold. Why did they have to be married this afternoon, what was the rush? Her mother had wanted to know. Sandi could be so uncooperative, she complained. Sandi did some quick thinking and devised the story that Steve was much too busy with important government business at this time to go flying off to California, even to get married there, and they didn't want to wait. Her main consolation was that it wasn't too far from the truth. "We'll fly out just as soon as Steve can arrange to be away, Mother. I promise." Sandi told her, keeping her fingers crossed that it would pacify her parents, at least temporarily.

To Sandi her grandfather seemed unusually uninterested. If she was happy that was fine with him. He spoke to Steve for a couple of minutes and told her when she came back on the phone that he looked forward to meeting him when they could arrange it. Then he changed the subject and told her the news about the ranch. Though Sandi was not prepared for her grandfather's attitude she did not have the time then to question it. There were too many things to do. The guests and minister would be arriving soon and she still had to dress.

A short while later Sandi stood in front of the mirror in the guest-room looking critically at her reflection. She wore one of the two dresses she carried with her on the bus. This one was a pale, baby blue, jersey that clung with intimate closeness to her slender figure. She would have preferred her other one, but it had looked a little worse for wear after being dumped unceremoniously on the floor of her bus. "Definitely not your everyday wedding dress," she commented to herself, "but then this isn't your everyday wedding either."

Sarah tapped lightly on the door before entering, "Everyone is ready downstairs. My, don't you look pretty? I can't tell you how happy we all are that Mr. Steve is finally getting married again, he's been alone for far too long now."

Again! Sandi only just stopped the word from escaping her lips. Steve had said nothing about ever being married before. I ought to have my head examined for thinking we can get away with this, I hardly know the man I'm supposed to marry in a few minutes.

"I tell you there isn't a man alive that can keep a secret as well as he can, why I hadn't a notion that you two had known each other for so long." Sarah continued without noticing Sandi's distress. "I can't think why he felt he had to keep you under wraps."

"He thought it best, you know how much Steve likes to avoid publicity." Sandi hoped that he did.

"That I do, my dear, that I do." Sarah seemed pacified with Sandi's explanation. The staff wanted me to express their welcome to you. They all think you'll make Mr. Steve a wonderful wife. Goodness, here I stand chatting away, you had better go down or they'll all think you've been kidnapped. You don't want to be late for your own wedding do you?" Sarah asked as she rushed Sandi out of the door, and Sandi thought, late no, I'd rather miss it all together. "Mr. Groiter is waiting at the foot of the stairs to escort you, it's a shame your father couldn't be here to walk you up the aisle himself. But I guess that's the way things work out sometimes."

The ceremony was relatively short but still had a profound affect on Sandi. She found herself wishing that the vows they took were based on real love, instead of make believe. Sandi had always wanted to be happily married with a couple of children to take care of. Somehow it had never turned out that way and this marriage, she realized didn't have a chance of surviving.

Sarah deserved a commendation for the delectable dishes she somehow managed to produce on such a short notice for the reception and buffet after the ceremony.

"Well, Mrs. Hoyt, is this so bad?' Steve bent down and whispered the question in her ear. The sensations his action produced made her want to melt in his arms.

"I don't think this is the time or the place to ask me that question," she replied softly with a glint in her eyes.

"Oh, I think it's the perfect time, with all these people around, I'm relatively safe," he grinned back.

"Are you giving the poor girl a bad time already, Steve?" an elderly woman who had been introduced to Sandi earlier as Steve's grandmother asked as she neared them. "Ignore him Sandra, he can be most obnoxious if he thinks he can get your dander up. He's been that way ever since he was a child, should have taken it out of him then, but we-all thought it was so cute.

"You're not being fair Granny," he knew she disliked that term. "Sandi is very capable of taking care of herself and if you two are going to gang up on me, I'll be forced to depart in self defense."

"Oh no you don't!" Sandi retorted quickly, grabbing his arm as if it were a lifeline. "You stay right here by my side." If he thought she would let him walk off and leave her at the mercy of all these people's questions he had a lot to learn about her.

"Listen to her, she can't bear to have me out of her sight," he teased.

"Humph," his grandmother snorted, "You invited all these people she doesn't know from Adam, while none of her own relatives or friends could attend, then threaten to leave her at the mercy of this bunch of nosy gossips. I think you're damn lucky she only grabbed your arm, if your grandfather had pulled a stunt like this, you wouldn't be here now, I'd have left him waiting at the alter!"

"I stand duly reprimanded and hereby promise not to leave her side for the rest of the evening, you're a witness."

By the time everyone had departed Sandi was not sure whether to be grateful or not for Steve's promise. True to his word he had not left her side, which may have protected her from having to answer some awkward questions, but it did nothing for her peace of mind. Having to stand next to him, often with his arm around her or holding her hand was too disturbing by far to her senses, and left her feeling exhausted and drained long before the last guest left.

CHAPTER NINE

Joey climbed off the plane feeling tired but more alive than he had felt in years. He had not realized just how much he had missed his old job. Admittedly this trip had proved fruitless, had in fact been a total waste of time, but somehow he felt useful again. He had not as yet seen Barbara, and his pride would not allow him to ask after her; still he thought of her and longed to see her and hold her in his arms. He wondered fleetingly what Sandi's reaction to their plan had been and whether she and Steve were married. Sandi would have gone along with it he decided, not without protest perhaps, but she was intelligent enough to know when to cooperate.

He had spent the last two days backtracking Nash's trail trying to pick up some clue 'as to what Steve was supposed to look at or for. Something perhaps to indicate why Nash had been so specific as to whom the list was delivered to. There was only one logical reason why, as far as Joey could determine, someone was working for both sides, the question was who? Nash must have known and had intended to tell Steve, unfortunately, he died too soon. Joey mentally ticked off the names of the people involved with the case, the President, Wayne, Steve, Barbara, Nash, and two other agents whom he had never met. The President he cleared without question,; Wayne, he had known for years, could he have sold out? Not likely he concluded.

It certainly wasn't Steve, regardless of any other reasons he was the one Nash had wanted the list delivered to. Barbara, he knew he was too close emotionally to her to make a rational decision, but it wasn't like the Barbara he had known in the past, he would stake his life on that bet. Nash had set this ball in motion and died in the process, so chances were it wasn't him. That left the two agents Joey didn't know. There could be others involved that he wasn't as yet aware of he realized, Presidential advisors, office personnel, maybe even other agents that Wayne had not mentioned. He decided to talk to Steve, alone, as soon as it could be arranged. It would take cold hard facts to make the agency suspect one of it's own, and if he wasn't careful he could wind up like Nash. With that cheerful thought, Joey hailed a cab and left the airport for Steve's home.

A single bare light-bulb hung over a dilapidated table around which sat six-men and one woman in an old abandoned warehouse on the waterfront some miles from Steve's home. The bulb's dim light shed eerie shadows around the hollow interior of the building.

"So what now?" the woman asked, "We can't afford to just sit back and do nothing."

"I don't intend to," one man retorted, his cold blue eyes assessing the rest of the group, "if this new information is correct, that little cowgirl has a photographic memory. I'll lay you odds that she looked at the list, a woman wouldn't be able to resist," he paused for just a moment, waiting for the woman sitting across from him to react to his last statement. He had meant it derogatorily and he could tell by her expression that she knew it, but she was wise enough to let it pass without comment. "Which means that all we have to do is get to her and persuade her to tell us what's on it," he continued.

"Sure Boss, and how do you propose that we do that? Hoyt's place is being guarded like a Fort Knox, it would be suicide to go waltzing in there," one of the other men spoke up.

"If you're a coward, you're in the wrong business Harry. I never said that it would be easy or that it wouldn't involve a certain element of risk. Nor did I suggest that we just go waltzing in there. As I see it there are a couple of different ways to get to her. If the first plan doesn't work, we'll use the second one. Now this is how it'll come, down...

Sandi absentmindedly began straightening up after the last guest left. It was a habit she had started years before, never liking to wake up to a messy house. "Leave that, Sarah will take care of everything in the morning," Steve told her.

"I don't mind, really, I'm used to doing things for myself. I hope you don't expect me to sit around and do nothing for the next several weeks, I'll go crazy."

"I'm sure that we can find something for you to do," he removed the cup she was holding from her hands. "But in the mean time it wouldn't look good if you were to try to take over the housekeeper's job. Besides, you look rather tired, you probably belong in bed. Come and sit down and have a night cap with me, I have a small problem I need to discuss with you before we call it a night."

"That sounds like a typical husband speaking," she quipped.

"Very funny, Mrs. Hoyt. I do hope you will retain your good humor while I present my dilemma to you."

"I shall make every attempt," she retorted, realizing that her present carefree frame of mind was probably the direct result of all the champagne she had consumed.

"You wouldn't by any chance have had a tiny bit too much of the bubbly would you?" he inquired as if picking up on her brain waves.

"Who me?" she returned with wide-eyed innocence. "I hardly touched the stuff."

"How enlightening, I'll have to remember that in the future."

"I thought we were going to have a night cap and discuss your problem, not examine my drinking habits for future reference."

"Ah yes... well, I don't quite know how to put this," he stalled, "it's rather delicate."

"Don't ask me, I don't have the foggiest notion of what you're talking about, so I can't tell you "how to put it'. However, I have found in the past that it's easiest to just, if you'll pardon the crude expression, sort of spit it out, when you have something to say."

"That might be the easiest, nevertheless, considering your sweet temper, which I have had the occasion to witness, I wouldn't want to do anything rash."

"Oh, so that's it, you want me to promise to keep my Irish temper in check, I should have known."

"Is that where you get it, your temper I mean?"

"Yes, and you haven't seen anything yet, I rarely lose my temper completely, but when I do look out. Now would you tell me what you want to say and get it over with? As you so rudely pointed out a few minutes ago that I looked 'rather tired', I think I should attempt to get some sleep tonight."

"Well..." That was all he managed before his phone began ringing, cutting him off. "Excuse me," he said as he walked to the phone.

"Saved by the bell," Sandi mocked after him, noting that he didn't seem very disappointed at the interruption.

The phone was at the opposite end of the room so she did not hear much of what Steve said, but by his expression, she could tell that he was not receiving the best of news. "I'll be right over," she heard him say loudly toward the end of the conversation, "No, I don't want to wait until morning, I want to see for myself, tonight?" He slammed the phone down before turning to her, "We'll have to continue this conversation tomorrow, Sandi, I have to leave for awhile."

If he hadn't looked so grim she would have said something to the effect that he needn't make excuses to leave her on their wedding night, instead she asked quietly. "Is there anything I can do, would you like me to wait up?"

"No; of course not; I don't know how long I'll be. It could take hours. Just go on up to bed and don't worry... wait...there is something, if Joey comes in before you go to sleep, would you tell him to come to the office, immediately."

"Sure, I didn't know he was coming back tonight," Sandi answered, watching him walk to the door. "Steve, is it something to do with the list, has something gone wrong?"

He stopped in mid-stride and turned to look at her, "Why did you ask that?" he demanded harshly.

"I don't know," his expression was so harsh and cold that it made her step back with surprise, "I don't know, I guess I just assumed from what you said. Steve, what's happened, can't you tell me? She was beginning to feel frightened now, a strange sense of foreboding was taking over her mind.

"If I can, I will, in the morning. Now get some sleep," he told her softly, his expression relaxing as soon as he saw her stricken face. He slowly walked back to where she stood, taking her by the shoulders he bent down and kissed her forehead gently, "Don't worry, Babe, I'm sure that it's just some sort of mix up, I'll take care of it. I'm sorry I frightened you."

She felt so safe standing there in front of him, his touch bringing her senses alive, but she knew it would only last until he walked out the door. It wasn't the first time he had taken the warmth of a room with him when he left it. She was beginning to recognize the feeling.

"Are you going to be okay? Maybe I should ring for Sarah."

"No, let Sarah rest, I'll be fine. Really," she added when he looked skeptical.

"If you're sure, I'd better get out of here." He turned and without a backward glance strode out the door.

Even though a short while earlier Sandi had felt exhausted she discovered that now she felt anything but. She determined that it would be impossible to sleep while in her present state of mind so she opted to wait up for Joey. Of course if Steve should return first she would not have regretted it.

Joey arrived only a few minutes after Steve left. "Hi." So much had happened since they had last seen one another that she was unsure as to exactly how to greet him.

"Steve had to go to the office, he said to tell you to go there too, immediately, if you came it,' "What's up?" he asked, also slightly unsure of himself.

"I don't know, Steve got a phone call and said that he had to leave and that he didn't know when he would be back." Her voice cracked somewhat at the last.

"Sandi, are you all right?"

"Fine," she chose the shortest answer she could give, knowing that her voice might betray her if she said more.

"Hey, this is Joey you're talking to Sweetheart" he walked over to her and slipped one arm around her shoulders, "Don't go giving me that 'fine' routine. What's really going on around here? Did you and Steve get married? Has someone tried to get to you or something like that?"

"I don't know what's going on Joey. We got married, this afternoon, as a matter of fact. I don't exactly know what's bothering me, I just feel like something terrible is about to happen... I can't explain it.

You're going to think I'm crazy, but it's like a premonition."

"Tell you what, I'll call Steve and tell him that I'm staying here with you, will that make you feel better."

"It's not me that I'm worried about, it's Steve. With all the guards around this place nobody in their right mind would try to get in. But they might try to get to Steve. Will you call me and let me know that he's all right when you get to the office? I know it sounds stupid, but..."

"Sure I'll call, I don't see that they would accomplish anything by getting Steve, and believe you me, Steve is very capable of taking care of himself. But I'll call just to put your mind at rest, okay?" He started to turn away, then turned back again as if something had just occurred to him, "You're in love with him, aren't you?"

"No!" she denied quickly, too quickly, "Oh... I don't know what I feel Joey, I'm sorry, I don't want to hurt you."

"Hurt?" he smiled, "I'm not hurt, I'm relieved, I won't take the time to explain now, just don't let it bother you anymore."

"You won't say anything to Steve, promise me Joey."

"It's not my place to say anything Sandi, besides I have enough problems with my own love life without taking on yours as well." He turned then and left, saying over his shoulder, "I'll call you when I get to the office, and don't worry, Steve can take care of himself."

"Don't worry," she muttered to herself, "don't worry, I wonder how many times I'm going to hear that tonight!"

It seemed like an eternity before the shrill ring of the telephone broke the silence. Sandi had been literally pacing up and down the room while she waited.

"Hello, Joey?"

"This is Nurse Smith at Walter-Reed Hospital; could I speak with Mrs. Hoyt?"

It took a second for Sandi to realize that it was she the nurse wanted. "I'm ... I'm Mrs. Hoyt."

"Mrs. Hoyt, your husband, Mr. Steve Hoyt, has been injured in an accident, he's asking for you, the doctor wanted me to call you and have you come as quickly as possible. I've arranged for a cab to pick you up."

"I'll be right there," Sandi answered, dropping the receiver back into place. Oh my God, I knew something was going to happen, I never should have let him leave. Please God, don't let him die, she prayed silently as she ran upstairs for her purse and coat.

The phone began ringing again as Sandi was running back down the stairs. "Damn," she muttered, dashing across the room to answer-it. "Hello."

"Sandi, Joey here, every..."

"Oh, Joey, I'm glad you called," she interrupted him. "Steve has been hurt in an accident, the nurse just called, I have to run, he's asking for me...

"Sandi," Joey broke in, "What are you talking about, Steve's here with me."

"With you?" she asked with disbelief. "But the nurse, she just called me."

"Sandi," Steve came on the line, "what's going on?"

"Steve, are you all right? She said: you were hurt, that you..." her voice faded when she finally began to comprehend that the call had been a hoax.

"Who said I'd been hurt, damn it girl, get a hold of yourself and tell me!" he ordered.

"A nurse from Walter-Reed Hospital just called; she said that you had been in an accident and that you were asking for me. Oh ... what else did she say? Something about arranging for a cab for me. I was just leaving when Joey called."

"Then thank the Lord he did! Obviously, the call was a hoax, I'm fine, do not, I repeat, do not leave that house. I'll call you right back in a couple of minutes."

There was a click and the phone went dead. She stood staring at it for a few minutes while the full meaning of what had almost happened to her sunk in. It didn't take a genius to figure out that someone was trying to get her away from the house and all the guards in order to grab her. The fact that they had tried it didn't bother her as much as the fact that they had almost succeeded.

Steve started to explain to Joey and Wayne what was going on while he dialed another number. "They were apparently trying to get her out of the house, they even went so far as to furnish her with a cab. Jerry?" he asked when someone answered the number-he dialed. "Steve here, do you see a cab there at the gate?"

"Steve, you okay? Yeah, a cabby just pulled up, said something about picking up your wife, that you'd been hurt."

"Arrest him I'll explain later." Steve heard the phone bang against some object when Jerry dropped it to do his bidding.

"Want to fill us in on what's coming down?" Wayne asked.

Steve spent the next few minutes recounting what he had learned from Sandi and explaining the call to Jerry, who was one of the agents standing guard at the front gate of his estate. "I'm calling Sandi back, and I'm going to arrange to have one of the guys go up to the house and sit with her. Unless I miss my guess she'll be too upset to sleep for awhile, and she shouldn't be alone. Any objections Wayne?"

"No ....Of course, not, if you want to go back there yourself I'll understand."

"I want to finish what we started here first." Steve replied, dialing his home number. "Sandi, this is Steve."

"I'm okay," she answered his as yet unasked question, "A little shook up, but I'll calm down shortly.

"I'm sending one of the agents to the house; I want him to stay with you until I get there. Try to get some rest; I'll be home as soon as I can finish up."

"It really isn't necessary, I feel like such a fool."

"Well don't, it was a trick anyone could have fallen for. And don't argue with me; for once just do as you're told. I have no desire to become a widower on my wedding day!"

"Yes sir," she acquiesced, not minding is commanding tone at all, this time.

"Good girl, I have to go, but I'll be home as soon as I can," and he hung up.

"I'm beginning to feel like I'm sitting in a rubber raft that somebody has been shooting at with buck-shot. I can't seem to keep up with all the leaks and it looks like the raft is sinking." Steve commented despondently, as he hung up the phone after arranging for one of the agents to stay with Sandi. "We'll all deserve a vacation if we can keep things afloat until those talks come up in a few weeks."

"Don't give up the ship yet Steve, there are too many people on-board. We have to keep things together." Wayne attempted to encourage him.

"You don't need to remind me. Let's go to the lab, we can fill Joey in on what else has been falling apart since he left on the way. And I'd like to hear what he found out, if anything."

"Joey, we have a slight problem with the list, it appears that part of it is missing, along with a considerable amount of microfilm," Wayne told him as they left his office for the lab.

"Any ideas as to where it is or what happened to it?" Joey inquired.

"Your guess is as good as ours, all we know is that when the lab boys decoded it, it appears that at least part of the list is missing, we aren't sure as to how much. You see we have no idea of exactly what Nash had come up with. But according to what we have, there should have been a list of names, along with locations of said people, and some pictures of them, and some of their equipment, so we could assess their power," Wayne explained.

"How much do we have?" Joey asked.

"As near as we can tell only some of the names, no pictures, and no locations"

"Do you think Nash may have stashed it somewhere?" Joey inquired.

"Possibly, that is, of course, one explanation."

"He has another, much more interesting one," Steve spoke up.

"Let's hear it," Joey prompted. "I may be totally off base….but I figure we have to look at all the possibilities. Maybe Sandi was given the complete list, maybe she's working with the other side."

"No way," Joey immediately defended her, "Steve you don't believe that do you?"

"My reaction was somewhat more explicit than yours, why the hell do you think I came running down here so fast. Wayne called me saying something about the possibility that I'd just married a spy and traitor."

"You two wouldn't be the first to be turned by a pretty face," Wayne maintained his stance.

"Wayne, I've known Sandi for quite awhile, it's not her style, she could no more play that game than I could fly. You're not only totally off base; you aren't even in the ballpark!"

"All I'm saying is that we have to admit that it's a possibility, we can't rule it out. To me it's mighty suspicious that she should be at some rinky-dink, cafe at the time she was. And I find it awfully hard to swallow that someone should just happen to make an attempt to kidnap her tonight, right after, we discovered a problem with the list. That's too coincidental to my way of thinking."

"I don't care how it looks to you, Sandi's not our pigeon," Joey stood his ground stubbornly.

"Do you have anything besides gut instinct to tell you that Joey?" Steve asked.

"No, but you can bet I'll find it, Steve, if it's the last thing I do."

"What did you come up with on your trip?" Wayne asked, trying to change to a less volatile subject.

"Nothing, a total blank, but that doesn't mean that I'll go along with your theory about Sandi."

They entered the lab and spent the next hour discussing the list and the different ways to approach their present dilemma. There was not enough time to redo all the research that Nash had done, somehow they would have to discover the whereabouts of the rest of the list. Joey said nothing about his suspicions of there being a double agent in their midst, deciding that the only person he would confide in was Steve. They had worked together with nothing but a hunch to guide them before, besides, Steve was the only one who seemed to agree with him about Sandi. He didn't really blame Wayne, Wayne didn't know Sandi and she wasn't cleared for top security the way his agents were.

They left the lab and returned to Wayne's office to question the taxi driver that Jerry had arrested at nearly midnight. It seemed that the poor man really was a taxi driver, he had been dispatched on what he thought was a routine call. When the dispatch operator was questioned he told them that he had received a call from a woman claiming to be a nurse at Walter-Reed, just as she had to Sandi. The question that was uppermost in everyone's mind was who the woman was, could it have been Sandi? Or was it perhaps Barbara, Joey asked himself. Or was it someone else? Apparently, Sandi was to have been taken to the hospital where someone would have been waiting to snatch her. An agent was sent to check out the hospital, but with little hope that he would find anyone. They were relatively sure that by this time whoever it was would know that their plan had failed.

When Steve and Joey were finally in the car together driving home Joey had his chance to talk.

"Well, what do you think?" Steve asked him, "you have that look on your face that tells me something is bugging you."

"Hell, I don't know what to think, the only thing can come up with is that there must be a double agent."

"Agreed, got any ideas?"

"I was hoping you would, you've been working on this longer than I have."

"Nary a one, to be perfectly honest, this has got me stumped. Did you really draw a blank on your trip?" "Yep, I didn't learn a single thing, except that Nash traveled over half of New York that night. After spending several hours pondering on this I have come up with a possible hypothesis however."

"So let's hear it."

"Mind you, this is strictly supposition. Let's assume that Nash knew that there was a double agent, and, his or her identity. It wouldn't be you; of course, you're the one he wanted the list delivered to. And it wouldn't be Sandi, or he wouldn't have given it to her to deliver. 'We can even take it one step further, suppose that he was trying to tell you where to locate the rest of the list when he died. That would explain the 'tell him to look', it doesn't answer the where, but it may be the what we are looking for."

"Sounds logical, you wouldn't want to speculate on the identity of the double agent, would you?" Steve asked hopefully.

"Not really, if this is all true, then it could be Wayne, Barbara, or anyone else that the list might come in contact with once it reached Washington. I don't even know who all the people are that are in on this thing, do you?"

"I'm not sure, let's check off the ones we do know. There is of course the President; I think we can safely clear him. Wayne, do you think he'd sell out?"

"A couple of hours ago, no, but now I'm not so sure, he tried real hard to make Sandi look guilty."

"True, okay, we'll do some checking on him. What about Barbara, you two were pretty close at one time, could it be her?"

"I've been wondering about her myself, it wouldn't be like the girl I knew, but people change. I haven't seen her in almost four years. We do know that a woman is involved." It hurt almost unbearably for Joey to have to admit that the girl he loved could be guilty.

"Then we'll have to investigate her too. That leaves Tom and Rick; you haven't met them yet, have you?"

"No, what's your opinion of them?"

"Instinct tells me they're straight, but then I feel the same way about Wayne and Barbara and we're going to check them out."

"Anyone else that you know about, has the President consulted any of his advisors, what about the office staff, has there been any correspondence on this?"

"As far as I know the President's been keeping this under his hat. There are the guys in the lab; I don't know who has access to the lab anymore. As far as office personnel, the only one I can think of that might know something is Wayne's secretary. But she's worked for the FBI longer than Wayne, you, and I all put together. It doesn't seem logical that she would swap sides now."

"Too true, tell me something, how'd you get involved in this thing Steve, I thought you gave this sort of work up when you became a senator?"

"It's a long story, I'll have to tell you about it sometime, but right now we're home," he turned the car into the drive and stopped at the gates. One of the guards opened the gates while Jerry came over to the car.

"Find out anything from that guy, Steve?"

"Not really, seems he is what he claims, a cab driver. Somebody called in and he was the lucky one who got dispatched out here."

"Well, maybe next time, we'll get a break. We won't be letting your wife leave here unescorted though. I've told the guys to keep an extra sharp eye out, after a trick like that you can't tell what they'll try next."

"Thanks Jerry, I'll see you in the morning, later today that is." Steve amended.

"Do any of these guys know why Sandi is being guarded so carefully?" Joey asked when Steve had driven on.

"We told them that someone is trying to either kidnap or kill her, not why someone wants to do it. It fits in well with the condition she and her bus were in when we brought her here and helped to make it believable. That's what my staff was told too."

"Well, it is the truth; you just left out a few details."

Steve had ordered Sandi to get some rest so many times that evening that she finally decided to do as she was told. He had enough on his mind, enough things going wrong, she reasoned, he did not need her giving him a bad time as well. He told her that he would explain what was happening in the morning, if he could, she would just have to curb her curiosity and wait until then. So much to Steve's surprise, he found that Sandi was already upstairs in bed when they arrived.

"I wish my wife was as understanding as yours Mr. Hoyt." Mark, the agent who stayed with Sandi told him. "She said you had enough problems without her adding to them and giving you a bad time too. Then off she went up to bed.

114

"Did she seem upset?" Steve inquired; he had been worrying about her all evening.

"She was pretty shaken up when I first got here, but after that, she settled down and seemed to be more embarrassed by the whole episode than frightened by it. Most of the women I know would have been hysterical; she was apologizing for causing so much fuss."

"That sounds like Sandi," Joey chuckled, "always more concerned for the other guy, than for herself."

"Apparently, that's what got her into this mess." Steve commented dryly.

"If you don't need me any more I had better get back outside, see ya in the morning," Mark said as he was leaving.

It was nearly dawn before Steve and Joey finally made their way upstairs to get a few hours of sleep, after spending several hours laying out a plan of action. It would not be easy for the two of them alone to do all the investigation that was necessary to discover who the double agent was and find the list in the amount of time they had, but somehow they would have to accomplish it.

CHAPTER TEN

Sandi awoke early the next morning and lay recalling the night before. She had not been asleep when Steve and Joey arrived home and had had to staunchly resist the temptation to return downstairs to satisfy her curiosity. For what seemed like hours she had lain awake waiting for them to come up, wondering what could be keeping them so long. Finally, drowsiness had overcome her, and she had fallen into a fretful sleep. Now in the light of day, she couldn't even remember what the dreams had been about, only that they had not been pleasant.

She climbed out of bed speculating on what the day held in store for her. I'm glad I'm not superstitious, she thought, I'd be racking my brain trying to figure out what I did to deserve this run of bad luck. Never in my life have I had so many things happen to me so fast. Maybe I shouldn't think of it as all bad... maybe I should count my blessings, she opened the window shades, noting the beautiful morning, it's gorgeous out and I'm still around to enjoy it.

Thirty minutes later she quietly left the house and made her way to the stable. She did not hear anyone stirring about in the house, so assumed that no one, not even Sarah had arisen. The sun, only just over the horizon, had not yet had a chance to dry the dew which still clung in shining crystal droplets to the leaves of the plants and grass. This was the time of day she loved the most, everything always seemed so clean and fresh. The only jarring note to the scene this dazzling spring morning presented were the two guards standing under a large tree. They acknowledged her with a nod as she walked down the path nearby which led to the stables. Their presence served to remind her of her circumstances and the incidents the night before, something she very much wanted to forget about, if only temporarily,

"How about a run before breakfast?" She asked Rap and Bubbles as soon as their exuberance from greeting her had settled some. She quite often rode early in the morning and could see no reason to change her habit; after all, the guards were still present.

Except for Rap's halter and lead rope all of her equipment was still in the side compartments of her bus. It would be much easier to take Rap to the bus, she decided, than to try to bring everything down to the stables.

For the next hour or so, Sandi worked Rap in the exercise ring. She longed to take him out onto the many bridle paths that bordered the estate and led down to the river but knew that it would be foolish as the agents would be unable to protect her.

"You're up bright and early this morning," Steve commented, walking up to the fence of the ring. "No ill effects from last night?"

"Good morning to you too," she smiled lightheartedly, for she found that she suddenly felt that way. "Not a one, it's much too beautiful out to carry a black cloud around."

"I couldn't agree with you more. Tell me, are you planning on joining us for breakfast?"

"If you'll wait while I put Rap away."

"Certainly, I'd much rather wait and have a beautiful face to look at over the breakfast table than not."

"Thank you, kind sir," she laughed down at him, wishing that he were serious, that he really thought her beautiful, the girl in the portrait was beautiful, but not herself.

"Mr. Steve, there's a call for you sir." Bill yelled out to him from where he was working in the stable. "Sarah just called on the intercom to let you know."

"Have her tell whoever it is that I'll be right there," he answered, turning back to Sandi, "Will you be long? Bill could put him away for you if you wish."

"I know where everything goes, I won't be very long." She turned and rode Rap to her bus to unsaddle him. As she was putting her saddle on its rack in the compartment she noticed a small scrap of paper laying on the floor. Where did this come from she wondered, picking it up? Seems to be a ticket of some sort, must have blown in when I had the door open. Shrugging, she dropped it into the pocket of a lightweight wind-breaker she was wearing to throw away later, promptly forgetting its existence because her mind was too full of thoughts about her husband.

Steve and Joey were both present at breakfast which was served in a small, glassed in room at the back of the house. French doors opened up onto the terrace were Sandi had eaten breakfast only the day before though with all that had been going on it seemed more like days before. Neither of the men mentioned the night before so Sandi began to think that she would never learn anymore about what had caused Steve to leave so suddenly. Instead they talked throughout the meal about old times and old friends that Sandi did not know. Rather than irritating her though, she found their conversation interesting, as she was able to learn more about Steve, who was fast becoming the center of the majority of her thoughts. Joey left immediately after breakfast, his destination unknown to her.

"Do you think we could depart to my study to finish that conversation we started last night?" Steve inquired as soon as Joey was gone. "You didn't have anything planned did you?"

For some reason beyond her comprehension or care his question about her plans annoyed her immensely. "And what, pray tell, would I have planned? Sandi asked him with sickly sweet tones. "I have no where to go, and you informed me last night that I should not do any housework. My time, it appears, is yours."

"I can see that I'm going to have to arrange for some sort of entertainment, all this idleness is doing nothing to improve your disposition." His tone led her to believe that she had perhaps over stepped.

"I'm sorry, I shouldn't have said that." He looked disbelievingly at her. "It was just the way you asked if I had anything planned, I really do appreciate all you've done for me, but you of all people should have known the answer to your question."

"Come on, there are a few things that need to be set straight. We can talk without fear of being overheard in my study."

Each time Sandi had entered Steve's study her eyes had been immediately drawn to the portrait of the lovely girl and Steve. This time was no different in that respect, however the portrait was not there. The wall was blank, the removal so complete and well done that she was left with the impression that she had imagined its very existence. There were no marks, nothing to show that it had ever hung there.

What happened to it? She asked herself.

"I thought it best that it be removed," Steve answered her unspoken question, leaving her wondering if she had unintentionally uttered her query aloud.

"I'm sorry, what did you say?" she asked, hoping that she had misunderstood.

"I noticed that you were looking for the portrait, I had it removed, I thought it best." He offered her no further explanation and Sandi was too embarrassed to ask for one. "Sandi, about...why are you blushing? You are the first girl I've seen blush in years"

"Am I? I.... I don't know, I guess it was because you noticed that I was looking for the picture." She decided the honest approach was the best in this case.

"Oh that, don't let it bother you, she's very beautiful, especially in the portrait, nearly everyone that comes in here looks at her. I just thought it should be removed as you are now my wife, it's really not important." Not important, I'll bet, Sandi thought while he continued. "Now, about last night, what I'm about to tell you is, well, there is no other way of putting it, it's a breach of security."

"Then why tell me, I'd rather not know if you'll get in trouble by telling me."

"If only it were that simple," he paused as if searching for the words to explain, "Joey and I are sort of breaking the rules, it's not the first time. As you know we used to work together, as a team, in the Navy and when we were discharged we worked for the government, all over the world. There have been other occasions when we didn't go by the book, I won't go so far as to say that we've always been right, but, we are still around to tell about them. At any rate, it seems we're back to doing it again. I won't pull any punches with you, if the wrong people find out, my career will be ruined and you will probably be in more danger than you are right now. Joey says you're straight and I happen to agree with him. He also said that you're a lot stronger mentally than most women, that you're up to taking the truth and helping out without falling to pieces. I sure hope he's right."

"I hope so too," she replied fervently, "but let me say one thing before you continue, don't tell me anything unless you're sure of me too Steve, I don't want you to doubt me or regret telling me anything."

"I wouldn't be here if that weren't the case, remember, I'm betting my career on you. It's up to you, you can take the safer way and stay out of it, or you can help us, probably increasing your own danger."

"But my helping will increase your chances of success? If I do it right of course."

"Yes," he replied softly.

"I'll help," she chose without hesitation while questioning her sanity.

"Joey said that you wouldn't hesitate, I guess he was right. Now then, last night, it was Wayne who called. Part of the list is missing, or maybe all of it, I'm not sure exactly how much or what. It may have been stolen after you gave it to me, or you may never have had it in the first place. Wayne seemed to think that maybe you stole it, that you're on the other side. Calm down," he interrupted her protest, "I wouldn't be here if Joey and I agreed with him. The first thing we need you to do is call on that fantastic memory of yours and reconstruct the list as you remember it. Can you do that?" She nodded, "Good, that will tell us whether or not it made it into Wayne's hands."

After furnishing her with paper and pencil Steve sat back and watched Sandi as she spent the next several minutes painstakingly reconstructing the list. As it was in code, it consisted of nothing more than a random bunch of letters, numbers, and words to her. Something of this nature was always the hardest to get total recall on so Sandi had picked out a pattern to be able to remember their order.

"Damn!" he said as soon as she had finished, "I was hoping we were going to have a quick and easy finish to this mess. If you had given me the whole list, it would have meant that someone took it after we sent it to the agency."

"Sorry, but that's all there was."

"It's not your fault; it's just that it makes things so much more difficult."

"Steve, how do you know that part of it is missing? Maybe Nash gave you all he had?"

"The first few lines here," he pointed to them, "It's in code, but basically it says that on the following pages," he pointed to where it supposedly said that, "we'll find a list of the top men in the resistance, along with their locations, pictures of their installations and info on their arms."

"The key word being pages, there is only one page."

"Right, where are the 'following pages', how many of them are there supposed to be? We just don't know, and there is not enough time to redo all the research Nash did before some very important meetings coming up in a few weeks."

"What does the rest of this say? If you feel you can tell me, that is."

"I'm in a little deep to worry about that now, its a few names and little about each one. Usually, the higher ups are listed first, then down the line in a report like this, but Nash apparently didn't do that this time. These names we've never heard anything about, so we think they must be some of the small guys, When you said pictures, did you mean of the regular photos or microfilm?"

"Microfilm, we haven't used that in years; it would probably be a thumb drive or a chip," She wondered if she had perhaps asked one too many, he seemed to be getting suspicious of her. "I read spy thrillers in my spare time. I don't know how realistic they really are, but I guess that's why I'm asking all these questions." She told him, hoping to relieve his mind.

"So what do we do now?"

"We wait until we hear from Joey, he's doing a little research. If necessary you may get the opportunity to play sitting duck." He made it sound almost like a treat that shouldn't be missed. "I'm hoping we can avoid it, but…" He left off, letting her draw her own conclusions.

"I see, I'm to be the bait to catch the fish."

"I don't want it to come to that Sandi, and if you want to back out we'll understand."

"Not on your life, besides the fact that this person, or persons, deserves to be caught, the sooner it happens, the sooner my life returns to normal." Her statement reminded Steve that he had very little time to enjoy her company; a look of displeasure crossed his face that Sandi didn't understand. "I will be out of danger if they're caught, won't I?"

"Probably, that is what we are hoping for at least. Joey and I think there may be a double agent, someone working for both sides. If so, it woult explain what Nash was trying to tell me to look for, it would also explain why he wanted the list delivered to me personally."

"Only he died before he could tell me," she stated bluntly. "Well, count me in, if I can help I'm willing, I can't be in much more danger than I'm in right now. I thought I was pretty safe here until that incident last night."

"Just remember, this is only what Joey and I think, no one else, not Wayne or the President, have the slightest idea of what we're doing."

"I just hope I can keep it straight in my mind, as to who knows what about what. It was bad enough with just one undercover operation, now you're adding another within the first. I have never been a very good liar, but I should become quite proficient by the time all this is over."

"You'll manage; Joey and I both have faith in you."

"The thing that bothers me the most is that you're jeopardizing your career. I'd never forgive myself if I did something wrong and you suffered because of it."

"At the moment that's the least of our worries, so don't let it bother you. Now then, last night I started to tell you about another problem."

"Ah yes....the delicate one," she smiled, remembering their conversation.

"That's the one, somehow it doesn't seem nearly as important now, but it is a loose end that needs to be tied up. I believe I explained that our marriage must appear real, not even the staff can suspect anything. That's going to be rather difficult if we're sleeping in separate rooms. Last night we got away with it, but only because you woke up early and left your room looking like no one had been in it last night." Her face was slowly losing color as she listened, she wasn't sure she wanted to hear what she thought he was going to say. "I went in to wake you up and found you weren't there, which gave me quite a scare I might add. Now don't get me wrong, I'm not suggesting that we really sleep together.""Then would you kindly explain what you are suggesting?"

"I'll take the couch, your room or mine, whichever you prefer. Just so long as we sleep in the same room and make it appear that we are sleeping together."

"I see," there was a lump in her throat blocking further speech. It was hard enough to keep her emotions under control seeing him this way, but sleeping in the same room, that could turn out to be next to impossible.

"I promise you, our relationship will remain entirely platonic, I like my partners willing; I won't force my attentions on you, no matter how attractive I find you."

The fact that he found her attractive came as something of a surprise and served to immediately change her outlook somewhat. She wondered what he would say if she told him that he might not find her totally unwilling. "Do you think that's fair?" She asked him after thinking for a moment.

"What's fair? That I don't rape you?" He asked with some astonishment.

"No silly, that you get the couch every night?"

"If you're suggesting that we share the bed, I'm sorry, but I can't make any guarantees about my behavior under those circumstances."

This conversation was doing wonders for her morale, he actually found her attractive! If she played her cards right maybe she could make him forget this other girl. She realized that falling into bed with him was not the answer, but the close contact of sleeping in the same room, though hard on the nerves it may be, might not hurt. "I was not suggesting that, only we swap off on who gets the stiff neck on the couch. Some where, I don't remember where, I heard that marriage is a partnership which requires a certain amount of compromise from both parties."

He burst out laughing, "Sandi, you're incredible, you really are. Here I am expecting all sorts of protests, and what do I get, your complete cooperation." He strode across the room and swung her into his arms, planting one of his brotherly kisses on her forehead. "Thank you."

Though his thank you kiss may have been intended to be brotherly the feelings it aroused in Sandi were anything but. Well, it's a beginning, she thought, reveling in the feeling of being held in his arms.

"One more thing," he stepped back, leaving her feeling totally bereft. "I personally don't like the idea of you leaving the house, but if you do want to go somewhere, shopping, or something like that, I want you to know that you are not completely tied here. All I ask is that you take a couple of men with you."

"There isn't any reason for me to go anywhere, unless you plan on doing a lot of entertaining. I'm afraid that my formal wardrobe is rather limited at the moment. Dresses are not exactly the norm on the rodeo circuit, so I don't carry many."

"Depending on how long all this takes we may have to do some entertaining, as well as attend a few functions, they're a necessary evil," he grimaced. "I'll open a checking account this afternoon for you, buy whatever you want."

"That is a very foolish thing to say to a woman, husbands never tell their wives to buy whatever they want, only what they need," she teased.

"I'm different; you may buy whatever you want, just be sure that you tell me if there isn't enough in the account, I don't want checks bouncing all over town. Of course, I wouldn't say that if I didn't trust you."

"Thank you, but really Steve, I can afford to buy my own clothes, I already have a checking account. You happen to have married a rather independent woman, who for the last few years has managed to support herself."

"I don't care how independent you are, or how capable of paying, you wouldn't be in need of clothes if it wasn't for the present situation. Don't argue with me Sandra," he ordered her sternly when she started to protest further.

Taking into consideration his furious expression and tone of voice Sandi decided that it might not be prudent to continue her protestations. "All right, I give; just don't think you're going to continue to get your own way all the time." She couldn't let him have the last word.

"I promise to let you have your own way, occasionally." he answered seriously, then added with a grin, "on unimportant issues of course."

"Thanks, I'm glad this isn't a permanent arrangement, I'm afraid if it were, we would spend a good portion of our time arguing."

"Probably, but think-how much fun we would have making up."
It's no use, she thought, he has an answer for everything.

"What, no come back?" he asked in mock horror, noting her expression he conceded, "Maybe I should quit while I'm still ahead."

"I think it would probably be a wise move on your part" she replied dryly.

"Sandi, all kidding aside, you will do as I ask in this won't you?"

"Yes, I want it on record that I protested, but I'll do as you ask."

"Do you really mind so much? I don't understand what the big deal is, most women would love to be given a free shopping spree."

"To quote you, 'I'm different'."

As if I hadn't noticed already, he thought before replying, "I know, you're independent, somehow I have difficulty picturing you like that."

"Oh really, how do you picture me?"

"Someday when this is all over with, maybe I'll tell you, right now I should be leaving. Just promise me that you'll be careful."

"Don't worry, I wouldn't consider being anything else but."

He left her there in his study wishing that their marriage was not a pretense. She stared unhappily down at the diamond encrusted wedding band he had placed on her finger the day before; the gems twinkled in the light. If only he loved me, she sighed, things would be so different. I wouldn't have protested at using his money, he would have kissed me good-bye, we would not have to discuss sleeping arrangements, and everything would be different. She went back over their conversation in her mind; there was still the question of who the girl in the portrait was? Sarah had said something about his being married before, could that be his first wife, was he still in love with her, what had happened? There was so little that she knew about the man she was married to and so much that she wanted to know. Joey had asked her if she loved Steve, did she? The wounds from her last attempt at marriage were still sensitive, leaving her hesitant to place herself in such a vulnerable position again. She didn't think she was ready to probe into the subject of 'love just yet, but on the other hand the attraction she felt for Steve was hard to ignore. Alan had told her that she was too childish and immature to love a man the way he needed. She would have to become more mature and sophisticated to attract a man like Steve, she decided. Until her meeting with him a few days earlier she had managed to put Alan's painful accusations to the back of her mind, avoiding thinking of them as much as possible, but now they seemed to haunt her night and day.

Steve found himself torn between delight and doubt at the results of their conversation. If he had the time he was certain he could get her to forget Joey, he was sure that she was already attracted to him, but at the same time the idea of stealing his friend's girl was abhorrent to him. The new sleeping arrangement could turn out to be either wonderful or regrettable, but at the very least, extremely trying on his nerves. He would be close to her, where he wanted to be, yet he would have to keep his distance. His thoughts chased themselves around in his mind like mice in a maze, leaving him confused and almost wishing that he had never laid eyes on one Sandra Stanford.

CHAPTER ELEVEN

Sandi threw herself into the project of moving into her new home. Though only a temporary arrangement, staying-busy afforded her less time to think about her present circumstances and therefore seemed to be her only hope of retaining some measure of sanity through it all. Refusing Sarah's help and taking time out to groom both Rapscallion and Bubbles however only served to delay the inevitable. She was finished by mid-day and wondering what more she could do to stay busy. Steve's intimation that he did not want her helping around the house, and that it would not be appreciated by Sarah either, left her baffled as to just what he thought she was going to do with herself all day. "I never thought I'd live to see the day that I couldn't think of a way to stay busy. Normally I have trouble finishing everything I set out to do. I'm like some poor little rich girl... Idle rich... poor little rich girl, she mused, the thoughts revolving in her mind like a childish taunt.

"When would you like to have lunch served Ma'am?" Sarah asked, coming up to her where she sat on the terrace. The question serving to only momentarily jolt Sandi from her derisive thoughts, while she wondered why

Sarah had become so formal toward her since her marriage. She decided that Steve must be right, Sarah felt threatened by Sandi's presence.

"Any time Sarah," she answered, smiling a trifle cynically and adding under her breath as Sarah nodded an acknowledgment. "At least it's something to do."

"Pardon Ma'am, was there something else?"

"Nothing," Sandi shook her head, "Nothing at all, I was only talking to myself." Sarah scrutinized her face. She liked this young woman, Lord knew there weren't many around worth a hill a beans these days, least not many that Mr. Steve knew, but this girl was different, and from the look on her face she was nearly at the end of her tether. "You know, if there's anything you'd like to talk about I'd be happy to lend an ear. Mind it'll not go further."

"Why thank you Sarah," Sandi was genuinely touched. After the recent formal treatment this was an unexpected turn around, and very nearly her undoing. She was so unprepared and unused to all that had been happening, Sarah had caught her at a weak moment, feeling alone and unable to cope. Thus the housekeeper's kindly offer brought an unnatural glimmer of moisture to her eyes.

"You know, I've never found that sitting about and moping did much good, far better to be busy."

"Ha!" Sandi laughed sardonically, "That's easy for you to say, you have plenty to keep you busy. You don't happen to have any suggestions as to what I might do with myself do you?"

"Why anything you'd like dear," Sarah was a bit mystified, "there are all sorts of things to do here, tennis, swimming.

"Oh Sarah," Sandi moaned, shaking her head, "the point is, I don't want to be entertained, as such. Lying about, swimming and playing tennis, etcetera, etcetera, are all fine, in moderation, but..." she paused, not sure how to explain so the older woman would understand.

"But they are all something you do in your spare time?" Sarah questioningly finished for her.

"Exactly, I'm so used to being busy, oh I don't know, this whole scene reminds me of, let's call it the idle rich, a mold which I do not fit into, and never have. It must seem a bit crazy to you, I can't really explain it, I know my Mother has always considered me to be a bit fanatical about this scene, but it's just the way I am.

"Crazy? I don't really think you are crazy, I think I can understand, after all you're just married and your husband goes off to work leaving you to your own devices in strange surroundings. You are used to going places, traveling, and taking care of yourself. This," she waved her hand expansively, "is a bit different from your bus. You have no friends or relatives nearby and of course those terrible threats on your life. Why don't you come along with me this afternoon? All the linen, china and silver used yesterday have to be stored away again. Some of it's quite old and delicate, I don't like trusting the regular help to take care of it so I do it all myself. Not exactly exciting, but it might help until we can come up with something better."

Sandi wondered just what Sarah had been told of her predicament and almost asked, then thought better of it, gratefully accepting the housekeeper's invitation instead.

While helping Sarah a short time after lunch she learned that one of Bill's assistants had quit a few days before, leaving him short handed and because of Sandi's situation Steve would not let him hire another just yet. With the spring growing season he was having a difficult time keeping up. Sandi quickly volunteered, gardening had always been a favorite pastime of hers, and this would be perfect.

Immediately, after finishing helping Sarah, Sandi, donned in gloves and old work clothes, proceeded to work in the flowerbeds, despite protests from Bill. The gardener seemed to hold some old fashioned ideas as to the actions of the mistress of the house. He finally went off shaking his head and muttering about what Mr. Steve would say should he discover his bride weeding. The last thing she heard him say was, "Likely fire me on the spot!" Sarah had forewarned her of what his reaction would be and Sandi had a fairly good idea of what Steve's would be, but decided that she would just have to jump that bridge if and when Steve did discover her diversion.

Working in the rich moist soil gave her a feeling of peace; the last few days had been so hectic. For the first time since the scene at the cafe she began to really relax, and found that she could mull over all that had happened in a relatively quiet and logical manner, with even a certain degree of detachment. The old saying marry in haste, repent in leisure came to mind as she contemplated her marriage to Steve, though she didn't know why. So far, other than being rather more cosseted than she really needed, she had nothing to complain about.

She had been at her task for only an hour or so when Steve's grandmother arrived. A distressed Sarah followed her out to where Sandi was working. "I'm sorry Ma'am; she wouldn't wait in the house while I sent for you."

"It's all right Sarah, don't concern yourself with it. Would you serve refreshments on the terrace in a few minutes?" Sandi calmly dismissed her, hoping Sarah would understand that her haughty tone was just an act. Turning to her guest she apologized, but not without noting her guest's arrogant expression. "I'm sorry, but I was not expecting company, If you'll excuse me for a few moments I'll go and wash up, then we can visit."

"Obviously you were not, but before we do anything, I wish you would explain to me why you feel it necessary to do the gardening? The last I heard my Grandson was far from destitute and retained a full staff."

Sandi took a deep breath and curbed her desire to tell the matriarch that it was none of her business. Head up and chin out she politely challenged. "Because I wished to, is there anything wrong with that?"

"Well, I'll be damned," the elder woman chuckled, completely unperturbed by Sandi's lofty attitude. "I thought you were cut from a different cloth than Steve's first wife when I met you yesterday, now I'm sure of it. I hate to be a nosy old lady, but what did Steve say about this?"

"Nothing," Sandi smiled mischievously, beginning to feel better toward her new relative, "he doesn't know."

"Ha!" His grandmother laughed, "Smart girl, I take it that you are not planning on enlightening him."

"Are you suggesting that he may not approve?" Sandi countered innocently.

"Well... let's just say that I don't think he would, I may be wrong of course.

"I seriously doubt it," Sandi replied dryly, "but if he thinks I'm going to sit around and do nothing but wait for him to honor me with his presence, he's in for a rude awakening!"

"I don't know why I'm poking my nose in, he undoubtedly knows you well enough to know how you feel already, and you do seem to be able to look out for yourself...I'm sorry dear, I shouldn't meddle. Steve is always telling me to quit trying to run everyone's life; they have to learn from their own mistakes."

Sandi shrugged, "I guess that's true to a point, but I don't think you're meddling. You've known Steve much longer than I have." She tried to forget that only a few moments earlier that was exactly what she had thought. "I think you're only trying to be helpful, Mrs. Hoyt."

"Thank you, you're a sweet child, but for Heaven's sake, call me Nan, everyone does, even Steve, when he's not being persnickety. Which reminds me, I had the Devil's own time getting in here to see you; they finally called Steve to get his approval. He'll probably be along soon, I can't for the life of me figure out why he seems to think you need to be protected from me, you're nothing like his first wife. There I go rambling on, you had better run along and change before he gets here. I'll have Bill put the tools away for you."

Sandi joined her a bare twenty minutes later. Half of that time had been spent in trying to decide what in her limited wardrobe she should wear. The majority of the clothes she carried with her in the bus were of jeans, t-shirts and western style shirts for competition, which though beautifully tailored somehow didn't quite fit the occasion or the status of a senator's wife in Washington, DC. I guess I am going to have to do as Steve said and go shopping, she thought, finally settling on a pair of white slacks and a lace trimmed green blouse that enhanced the brilliancy of her eyes.

Nan did not mention Steve's first wife again, much to Sandi's disappointment, but neither did she ask any awkward questions, which was a relief. She seemed genuinely interested in Sandi's life as a professional rodeo contestant and encouraged her to talk about her life before marrying Steve. She was completely entranced by Rapscallion, who nuzzled her lovingly when Sandi took her out to see him.

"He always wants to be the center of attention and is the biggest show-off there ever was. He's more like a little kid than a horse," Sandi explained after Rap nickered and fussed when they left him to walk back up to the terrace. Bubbles, who was now finding her way around the estate and discovering which members of the staff she could bribe into giving her attention, followed quietly along. She still preferred her mistress, company whenever she could have it.

"I used to dream of, living on a real ranch when I was a child, horses have always fascinated me. But time and other obligations got in the way of my fulfilling that dream and now I'm a bit too old to take up riding," Nan sighed.

"It can be a dangerous sport, but with a good horse, there isn't any reason you couldn't learn to ride if you want to. My grandfather rides all the time, of course he has ridden for years', but I've met people who started later in life and never regretted it."

Steve arrived home, as predicted, a short while later, to find them visiting like old friends. He greeted them both, kissing his grandmother on her cheek, before turning to Sandi. He had taken her in his arms and placed a brief but sensual kiss on her lips before she could even begin to protest, which she had little desire to do. It was over just as quickly, leaving her feeling shaken and tingling, while Steve casually sat down in-the chair next to hers. Sandi was aware that the kiss was only part of the charade, however, the effect it had on her senses was definitely not, and proved more that just a little difficult to ignore. Every nerve in her body cried out for more contact with him, while he sat seemingly totally unaffected by her presence. This is absurd, if I keep this up it won't be long before he guesses how I feel, she admonished herself, summoning the will power to turn her thoughts away from the masculine frame lounging next to her and back to the conversation at hand.

"I would like to hold a dinner party in a few weeks, I thought it might be wise to send out invitations now," Nan was saying.

"Since when have you asked my advice on sending out invitations?" Steve asked while finding himself unable to entirely dismiss the impression of Sandi's lips on his. He wondered if his grandmother was deliberately being deluding or if he was so distracted by Sandi that he was being obtuse.

Since I thought that you might like to have a little peace and quiet. You said yesterday that you couldn't get away for a honeymoon right now. I thought you would enjoy some time alone here, perhaps I was wrong?" Nan noticed that she did not have either one of the newly weds complete attention.

"On the contrary, I would enjoy it very much," he was still mystified as to what she was getting at. "But you'll have to pardon me, I fail to see what your dinner party has to do with our being alone."

"I will word the invitations so that it will appear that my party will be Sandi's introduction into Washington's society. If handled properly, no one will have the nerve to bother you with any other invitations until after... it would be a direct insult to me."

He knew that if anyone could accomplish it, Nan could, he just wondered why he hadn't thought of it himself. "Sounds fine to me, what do you think, Sweetheart?" He turned to Sandi who was still having trouble following the conversation because of his distracting presence.

"Me...it's up to you, darling, whatever you prefer." She recovered herself quickly, not sure what it was that she was leaving up to him.

Nan left a short time later, explaining that she did not wish to intrude on the young couple's time together.

She had accomplished what she had set out to do. The day before they hardly appeared to be in love, much less know one another. Now she felt certain that they were in love, though whether or not they were aware of it was another question, why they had chosen to marry was unimportant, just so long as they were in love. She chuckled inwardly thinking it would prove interesting watching them discover the fact.

"Sorry about that," Steve apologized as soon as they were alone.

"About what?" Sandi asked, wondering what else she had missed.

"I was in a meeting when I learned she was here to see you. I came as soon as I could get away, I hope she wasn't too difficult to handle."

"Not at all," Sandi shook her head, "I like her, she reminds me of my grandfather, I guess it's because neither one of them is as pretentious as they lead people to believe."

"The feeling must be mutual', she never welcomed Karen like that. A dark expression flashed so fleetingly across his face that Sandi thought she might have imagined it before he changed the subject. "I told my secretary I'd be out for the rest of the day, I thought you might like to get away from the house for awhile, maybe take a drive, go shopping, name your tune."

"It's getting pretty late to go shopping, though I did take an inventory of my wardrobe and I guess I'll have to fill in a few blank places fairly soon," she admitted. "But I haven't been to Washington since I was a little girl, I don't remember very much, so, I think I'll pick going for a drive, if you're sure it's safe?""I shall do everything in my power to assure it, he glanced at his watch, "If we leave right away perhaps we'll have time to do some of each."

They left a few minutes later, after Steve arranged for them to be followed by a couple of the agents whom Sandi had dubbed her guardian angels. "We're taking a chance here, but I stacked the deck, in our favor of course," he told her when she commented about their escorts.

Sandi found the traffic in the city to be more than just slightly unnerving at first. People had a tendency to swerve suddenly, or just plain stop without warning, to gawk at different points of interest. Steve seemed accustomed to it, though he had said they would have to hurry he never showed any signs of irritation at the impediment of their progress, so she soon relaxed and sat back to enjoy herself.

She wondered what Karen had been like, apparently she was his first wife, and Nan had not gotten along with her. But Steve seemed to have some rather unpleasant memories of her too. Could she be the girl in the portrait? If it bothered him to think about her, then why keep a picture of her around? But if it wasn't Karen in the portrait, who was it? There were so many questions Sandi wanted to ask, but did not feel she had a right to. They were married, but in name only, she was not really his wife, in the true sense, which was exactly what she had agreed to, but then she hadn't planned on getting emotionally involved with her husband.

Steve took her first to a small, but clearly an exclusive dress shop on a back street in town. She was given little time to dwell on the fact that he was not only recognized but apparently a well known and valued client. In a madcap whirl dresses and accessories were brought out for her to examine, try on and choose from. She had seen and worn enough expensive clothing in her time to know that the next step up from these ready-mades, were custom designer models. There were no prices on the merchandise so the management must have followed the philosophy that if you have to ask you can't afford it. Whatever the bill was for the several dresses and accessories, most of which Steve had chosen and decided that she needed, she didn't know, but that it would have, at the very least made a sizable dent if not completely drained her own account she was sure. After arranging for everything to be delivered the following morning, they were on their way for what Steve described as a mad dash tour of the city.

He proved to be an excellent guide, taking her first to the Lincoln Memorial, then proceeding to the Thomas Jefferson Memorial and the White House, pointing out anything he thought might be of interest to her along, the way and telling her interesting trivia or the history of a building. Though she could only view it all from the car, as Steve decided that it would be pushing they're luck too far to go walking about, she enjoyed herself to the limit. It was dark before they reached the Capitol, Steve assured her that seeing it lighted at night was one of the best times, and she wasn't disappointed. From its base to the top of the Statue of Freedom on the dome, it was one of the most impressive sights she could ever remember seeing. Any patriot could not help but be touched by it, and Sandi was not immune.

"Are you by any chance getting hungry?" he asked her as they left the capitol behind, "I told Sarah that .we might eat out, if you felt like it. I know of a nice, quiet little place, the food is some of the best around and security shouldn't be a problem."

At that moment, she would have agreed to most anything he suggested. It crossed her mind that he was being very attentive, that perhaps it was all part of the act, but she was enjoying his company far too much to delve very deeply into his motives.

The restaurant, when they reached it was everything he had promised and more. It was not just nice and quiet, it was intimate and romantic. Soft music played in the background, while couples sat at candlelit tables placed far enough apart to allow for intimate conversation. A few swayed slowly to the music on the postage stamp dance floor in the center of the room. At first Sandi wished that she had changed into one of her new dresses, rather than having them all sent to the house, but it soon ceased to bother her after a few of Steve's compliments. "I shall have to make a habit of this, Mrs. Hoyt," he whispered softly in her ear, sending thrilling chills down her spine, as they were being led to their table. "It's good for my ego to be seen with a girl that turns all the men's heads when she enters a room."

She kept telling herself that his comments were nothing more than pure flattery, but that didn't stop the funny feeling in the pit of her stomach that they gave her. She knew tomorrow she would probably regret this evening, but she didn't want to think about it at the moment. Rational thought had long since given way to the dizzying pleasure of the romantic evening they were sharing. Afterward, she could not even remember for sure what she had eaten; only that it had been delicious.

All good things it seems must come to an end and the evening was no exception. The one and only time they danced was after dinner. Sandi began to wonder if there was anything that Steve did not excel in-and told herself that she would have to thank her mother for insisting she take dance lessons. It was heavenly to be held so close, so safe, and secure in his arms, their bodies molded to one another as if they were made for just each other as they floated rhythmically to the slow sensuous beat of the music. But when the music died down the magic spell that seemed to have held them throughout the evening died.

Steve suddenly became impatient to leave, his attitude changing from that of a romantic partner to that of a cold stranger in a split second. He said little, offering her no explanation, so she spent the time it took for them to drive home sitting quietly on her side of the car asking herself what she had said or done wrong. Perhaps he had guessed her true feelings for him that she was not acting. Then she berated herself for her own stupid actions. She could not gather the nerve to question him, too afraid that his answer would only confirm her suspicions. So she sat quietly, staring out the window, torturing herself with her thoughts.

He suggested that she go on up and prepare for bed when they arrived home, he would be along in a few minutes. She had chosen to use his room, rather than have him move, when she had moved into the house that morning, now she almost regretted the decision. The pillow she laid her head on smelled faintly of his after-shave and tobacco from the cigarettes, which he occasionally smoked. Silent tears coursed down her cheeks and onto the offending pillow while she lie in bed waiting for the muffled sound of his footsteps on the carpet announcing his arrival. Finally, after what seemed an eternity, he came in, treading almost silently as he moved toward the couch. She heard him shuffling about, getting undressed and settled, then he seemed to fall almost instantly asleep. Sandi listened to his rhythmic breathing, trying to relax and will herself to follow suit, but sleep was elusive. Steve's cold rejection of her brought the terrible memories of Alan and Peter back, so it was near dawn before she ultimately slept. Even then it was restlessly and filled with nightmarish dreams of the past.

CHAPTER TWELVE

A quick glance around the room told her that she was alone; Steve was gone, leaving behind no visible traces of his presence in their bedroom. Only the unmistakable aroma of his after-shave hanging in the air served as the solitary unwelcome reminder of his recent proximity. Chilling discouragement washed over her as the memories of the disastrous end to their evening came flooding back into her consciousness. Feeling totally depressed and emotionally mauled Sandi climbed out of bed muttering and attempting cheerfulness in spite of her dispiritedness. "Well, at least he's neat and I don't have to go about picking up after him."

She dawdled with her toilette, reluctant to face Steve again, his cold rejection the evening before, still fresh in her mind, left her disinclined to face a repeat performance. Her efforts were unnecessary however, as Sarah told her that Steve had left the house hours earlier when she finally gathered up the courage to go downstairs for breakfast. After gearing her mind up to facing him, it was an irritating anti-climax to discover that he wasn't even there.

Sarah served her, quietly noting that the new Mrs. Hoyt did not appear to be in any better mood than her husband had been in before leaving. The couple was apparently not experiencing wedded bliss, she thought. But was it any wonder, they had no time to themselves, no honeymoon and all this turmoil with break-ins and threats. She shook her head sadly, wishing there was some way she could help these two people, she cared so much about, find the happiness they deserved.

Sandi forced herself to swallow the food set before her, though its taste resembled dry sawdust and it kept sticking on the lump that seemed to have taken up permanent residence in her throat. Aware that moping about would not serve to change things for the better, improve her mood, or make the time pass any faster, Sandi went out and exercised Rapscallion and played with Bubbles before resuming her task in the flower beds that she started the day before.

She worked without stopping for the rest of the day. Sarah tried to get her to break for lunch, but she refused, the thought of food still sickened her. Even the arrival of her new clothes did not bring her away from her undertaking. It was nearly dark when she finally gave up and went inside, Steve had not yet returned and there was no word from him. The evening stretched out before her, long and lonely. Desire to see him, to know that he was all right, had long since replaced her desire to avoid him. Where is he? What's happened? The questions repeated themselves over and over, like a broken record in her mind. She tried reading after making a half-hearted attempt at eating dinner. When that failed to distract her, she tried watching television, only to find herself listening for the sound of his car, or staring at the phone as if willing it to ring, unable to follow the story on the screen any better than the one in print.

Feeling frustrated and near tears she vowed to wait up and have it out with him. But she had not taken into account her exhausted condition. Topping off several days of mental stress with poor rest, hard physical labor, little nutrition and more mental stress did not leave her capable of sitting vigil. So even though she was worried and upset it was not long after she turned off the television and curled up in a comfortable over-stuffed chair that her lids drooped and she was soon fast asleep.

Steve found her there when he came in a few hours later, the soft light from a single lamp bathing her in its golden glow. With sleep erasing all the signs of worry from her face she appeared to be little more than a child, soft and vulnerable, in need of protection. A craving, that unsatisfied became a physical ache, welled up and spread through his body for her touch, to hear her voice, see her smile, kiss her lips.... to feel her body melt against his hard frame as it had the evening before. Stop it you fool! She doesn't want you; she's in love with Joey! He turned abruptly away to the cabinet where the liquor was kept. How many times have you told yourself that today? He silently sneered at himself, while pouring a generous helping of bourbon into a glass, who are you trying to kid, you've been telling yourself that ever since you laid eyes on her! He drained the glass in one swallow, feeling the liquor spread its fiery warmth through him while pouring another.

The second drink he carried to the chair opposite the one Sandi was curled up in, slumping down, half sitting half laying he wondered if he should wake her, leave her where she was, or try carrying her up to bed. It was a difficult decision, he knew that to touch her might finish off what will power he had left, holding her on a crowded dance floor the evening before had very nearly been his undoing, yet he wanted to hold her so badly. Sandi's lashes fluttered as she slowly awoke, relieving him of the burdensome determination.

"Oh!" she exclaimed, sitting up suddenly when she saw him, "I must have dozed off; I didn't know you were home."

He smiled all of the tension he had felt at the prospect of their next meeting melted away. "You're very precious when you're sleeping." Sandi felt her color rise, wondering just how long he had sat watching her. A half chuckle escaped him. "You're blushing again, it's so unusual now days," his voice was soft and wondering, almost hypnotic, not teasing or belittling as she expected. "I like it," he continued, "too many women seem to have lost the desire to be feminine...ERA and all that, they seem to have become hard and cynical, feeling that they have to compete with men on their own level...but you don't do you?"

"I never really thought about it," She answered in a quiet tone, noting his tired and drawn face, the, as yet, untouched drink in his hand. She longed to reach out and touch him, to find a way to soothe his harried soul, instead she simple stated, "Men are men, women are women, everyone man, woman, or child, steps to the beat of their own drum."

The ingenuousness of it struck a responding chord somewhere deep inside him, though he wasn't sure why. It

159

just seemed to sum up Sandi's whole outlook on life, the simplicity of it to some might have been laughable, but not to him, not then, not ever.

They reached out mentally to one another, forcing the outside world and all of its problems into another dimension that for the moment did not exist. How long they sat and talked or exactly when she had fallen asleep cuddled up in Steve's arms on the sofa Sandi could not recall. The fact that they had not discussed their future, or for that matter, their feelings for each other did not bother her in the least; all that mattered to her was that they had gained a tenuous hold on something very, very precious. She snuggled closer, basking in the warmth and comfort his arms afforded. Loathe to open her eyes, afraid to expose their new relationship to the light of day, afraid it would lose its dream like quality and vanish as the morning dew does with the rising of the sun, Steve felt Sandi shift slightly closer, so he knew she was waking. Even though one arm ached almost intolerably, and the other had long since lost all feeling, he was reluctant to speak and break the spell that held them. He too, felt they had crossed a momentous bridge in their relationship. At the moment he could not even recall for sure how they had gotten from separate chairs to the sofa, only that it all seemed very natural. Perhaps Sandi would never love him as he did her; he dared not even hope for that, it would be enough if she were happy...no matter whom she was with. Noble thoughts to be sure, but as is the case with most things, much easier said than done, for he had not accounted for the greedy, green eyed monster, jealousy.

CHAPTER THIRTEEN

Joey had learned some very-interesting facts about Wayne and Barbara. The only problem was, none of them were particularly encouraging.

Wayne was heavily in debt, which was a possible motive for selling out, if he had. Joey didn't know the reason behind his present position, but it probably didn't matter anyway.

Barbara, he learned, was not married, that was the sum total of the good news. She was seen regularly in the company of a man who appeared to have no background or at least none that was readily discernible. It was hard enough on him to learn that she was dating someone regularly, someone she could be seriously involved with, but to not be able to find out anything about the man was considerably worse. "Who is he?" He asked himself for the umpteenth time. Could he be connected with the case, perhaps operating under an assumed name? Does Barbara know who he is, or is the man using her? He hated to even think that she might be the woman that had called Sandi pretending to be from the hospital, yet he had to admit that it was a definite possibility.

He needed to talk things over with Steve; he wished that somehow one of them could gain access to the agency computer, without anyone finding out about it. That would be a trick to end all, might as well wish for a miracle.

He wondered what Steve had found out about the other two agents, if just one of them could be cleared it would give them another body to do some of the legwork.

What day was it? He shook his head trying to clear it. He was tired, so tired that twenty-four hours sleep would seem like a short nap. He could not even remember the last time he had slept a full night in a regular bed, must have been Tuesday, the night of Sandi's wedding, no, that had been a short night too. He smiled at the thought of Sandi finally falling for someone. She was a wonderful person and he hoped that she would at last find happiness. He would have to talk to her though, explain why he was so happy that she had found someone, especially when that someone was Steve. They made a good couple.

For the fourth time, in as many minutes he noticed the lights of the cars coming at him start to blur. He shook his head again, trying to clear his vision and his mind. He had gone too long, he had to be careful, his mind was wandering, and he wouldn't be any good to anyone if he fell asleep at the wheel and killed himself.

Sandi sat reading, waiting for Steve to come home, he had left right after breakfast and she had not seen or heard from him since. He had told her that he might be late, for her not to worry; there was so much he had, to do. All day she had been floating on air, maybe Steve didn't love her, but he was not immune to her either, and that was definitely a beginning.

After dinner, she had thought about watching the television but there was nothing on to interest her so she went into the study to see if she could find a book to read. Two walls of Steve's study were completely lined with books, there must be something here somewhere that's interesting, she thought.

Dickens to Shakespeare, history to fantasy, science to poetry, it was all there. She picked out a few and was about to turn away when a small, nondescript book with an extremely worn cover caught her eye, Manuel for the Solution of Military Ciphers. This might be interesting, she decided, especially under the present circumstances. She had done a small amount of study on deciphering codes; people with her 'gift' were supposed to be good at that sort of thing. She had never thought herself particularly exceptional at it, but then, she had never had any great incentive before.

It was this book that Sandi was thoroughly engrossed in when Joey arrived. If he thought he felt bad he should have looked in a mirror. A couple of days growth of beard added a shagginess to his obvious tired condition, his eyes, sunk into dark, blue-black sockets, were red rimed, he even appeared to have lost weight. Sandi had never seen him look even remotely as bad as this. "Joey, what happened; are you all right?" She jumped up and ran to him, her book forgotten.

"I'm fine, just tired, where's Steve?" He looked around noting the room was empty.

"He hasn't come in yet, I don't know where he is, or when to expect him, he said it would probably be late though."

His stomach growled reminding that sleep was not the only thing he had missed lately. "Do you think a guy could get something to eat around here, I know it's late, but I sure could use a snack...something...anything."

165

"Of course, Sarah's already out for the night, but I'll get you something. How about an omelet, it's quick?'

Fine, I'll go attempt to make myself presentable," he scratched his beard, "If I look half as bad as I feel it's a wonder you recognized me."

Slightly less than twenty minutes later, Sandi scooped a fluffy ham and cheese omelet onto a plate and set it on the nearby kitchen table as Joey walked in looking considerably better.

It bothered her that he was going through so much for her. He was obviously exhausted, it just was not fair, he had told her not to concern herself anymore with his feelings for her, yet he was nearly killing himself to help her. Why, oh why can't I love him? She asked herself, love is such an unpredictable creature, doing as it wishes, without a thought as to what is right or wrong, who will be hurt and who will not.

"Just in case you aren't aware of it, you are a fantastic cook, this is delicious." Joey complemented her while almost wolfing down the food.

"Thanks, but I think from the way you're going at that nearly anything would taste good to you right now," she teased him.

166

"You're probably right," he replied dryly with a wink, "Sandi, all joking aside, I have to talk to you about us. The other night, I didn't mean to make it sound as though I didn't care about you at all."

"Oh Joey, I know you didn't..."

"Let me finish, a long time ago, before I bought the ranch, long before I met you, there was someone else. Someone here in DC that I was in love with...and well ... to make a long story short, I guess I'm still hooked. I hope you understand, I care about you very much, and if you had agreed to marry me, I never would have done wrong by you, but..."

Sandi smiled, nothing could be better as far as she was concerned, as long as he was telling her the truth. "Joey, you wouldn't just say that so I wouldn't feel bad would you?" she asked bluntly.

"Hell no! We're better friends than that, aren't we? "

Sandi wasn't sure what being friends had to do with it, but she did so want to believe him. "We sure are," she said throwing her arms around his neck and kissing him, too delighted to contain herself. "Oh Joey, you don't know how much better this makes me feel."

Of course Steve could not have walked in a few moments earlier and heard the first part of the conversation, or a few moments later and missed it altogether. All he heard was Sandi saying something about being ecstatically happy as she threw her arms around Joey's neck. It was very plain to him that they had come to some sort of agreement to put their relationship on the back burner until the present situation got sorted out. Never one to make a scene, especially under the present circumstances, Steve swallowed his pride and his pain.

"Tell me does the errant husband get one of, those too?"

"Steve!" Sandi's face lit up at the sight of him, but he didn't see it, he was too busy looking away, still trying to hide the stabbing pang that he felt sure must show in his eyes.

It never occurred to Sandi that Steve knew nothing of Joey's feelings for another girl, nor did she realize that he was under the mistaken impression that she was in love with Joey. Therefore she saw no reason to explain her action, even though it was a little aggravating that he didn't seem even slightly jealous, after all he had walked in and found her with her arms around another man, his best friend no less. She wished that there would have been at least some-comment, some censorship, something, anything to show that he cared, anything other than this friendly joking and kidding.

CHAPTER FOURTEEN

Sandi slipped into a routine of sorts as the days drug slowly by. Over the past few weeks there had been an almost un-perceptible change in Steve. He remained unfailingly polite, but at the same time he seemed distant and remote, almost cold. They were rarely in the company of others so it was seldom necessary for him to play the roll of loving husband. She couldn't decide which was worse, his cold courtesy or fake fondness, but finally settled on cold courtesy, at least it represented his true feelings, or so she thought. There were moments, when he thought she didn't notice, that she would catch him studying her, a strange unreadable expression in his eyes. Those were the times she would feel the most drawn to him, but any advance on her part would always cause him to withdraw behind his cold mask. Unfortunately because of this impasse she remained woefully uninformed about the case. She didn't know if things were improving or worsening. How or where Joey was, whom she had not seen or heard from since the night he had shown up looking half dead, or for that matter, how much longer this charade was to continue. Though often tempted to inquire as to how things were proceeding Steve had only to turn his cold stare upon her, one look would quell her curiosity like water on a fire.

She filled the long and lonely hours by helping both inside and out around the estate, and studying the book of ciphers. There was something about the list that bothered her, but as yet the "what" remained elusive. To her knowledge Steve had never discovered the fact that she was helping Sarah and Bill, or if he had, it hadn't mattered to him.

The day dawned cloudy and cool, it was apparent that spring showers would be the order of the day. Sandi was sorely tempted to rollover and go back to sleep, but Rapscallion and Bubbles would be waiting for their breakfast and Bill would not be there to feed them. She had given Sarah and him the day off to visit their daughter and her husband and see their new granddaughter. That meant she would have to feed her own animals and take over for both of them today, not that they had left her all that much to do. "If they keep waiting on me all the time, I'm going to be royally spoiled," she muttered, throwing back the covers and sitting up. "I never used to even think about staying in bed."

The couch was empty, as usual, no matter how early she awoke, Steve had always already left. She wondered briefly how he managed to keep up the pace. He had steadfastly refused to allow her to sleep on the couch, though she had offered several times. She even thought about defying him and getting there first, but the memory of his chilly gaze always killed the idea.

A short, terse note was taped to her mirror. It was not the first time Steve had chosen this form of communication and it never failed to irritate her to the core. This time being no exception.

Dinner tonight, be ready *by 5:00.*

Steve

"Yes sir!" She gave a mock salute, of all the unmitigated nerve, he takes the cake....dinner...dinner wherewith whom...formal...informal? She fumed, crumpling the note and tossing it into a handy waste basket. Her present circumstances were getting on her nerves, more so each day and at the moment she felt like telling him and all his cronies, including Joey, to go to bloody hell!

Smoke hung in a constant never ending haze in the small bar, Even though it had just opened for the day the air reeked with stale smoke, stale liquor and to the tall, impeccably dressed man with ice blue eyes, stale bodies. His nose crinkled slightly with distaste, he had always avoided these dens of decadence, he was above this sort of place. Unfortunately the individual he was about to meet was not.

There was only one customer in the place, he sat back to the wall, in a rear booth, his tawny, cat like, cunning eyes seemed to take in everything with a glance. El Lobo, the Boss knew him only by reputation, but that was enough.

"You are the one they call the Boss? El Lobo asked in a soft raspy voice, as he approached the table.

"Yes, I've brought what we agreed on," he tossed a plain white envelope on the table. "Count it if you wish, it's all there, the job must be finished within the next twenty-four hours, or the target will have left the area. The rest of your payment will be waiting for you, as we arranged."

"It will be done," he stated simply, nodding his head in a way that indicated the Boss' time was up.

The Boss turned and strode out of the bar without a backward glance. El Lobo was one of the few men who could make him nervous; the man could kill his own grandmother without turning a hair.

Joey jumped into the car before it had stopped completely.

"What's so important?" Steve asked before he got the door closed.

"The name El Lobo ring any bells?"

"Loud ones, he's one of the best mechanics around, when he goes after someone you might as well start making the funeral arrangements."

"Yeah, well guess who's in town? Joey asked, sounding totally defeated and tired.

"Why, who's he after?" Steve asked, afraid he already knew the answer.

"I don't know for sure, I lost him about an hour ago, that's why I called you, there are two people I can think of right off hand, Sandi and the President. With all the info we've been dropping around somebody is bound to be getting worried. Wish we could get that little pip-squeak we nailed snooping around the estate the other night to talk. I don't know, Steve, I thought they would try to kidnap her, but maybe we pushed them too far. They may have decided that she's better off dead and telling no one. And ya know, there is the remote possibility that his being in town has nothing at all to do with this?"

"I know, this is just great," Steve shook his head; "Do you have any idea how happy that makes me?" He asked sarcastically.

"Hey, I'm on your side, remember. I thought you should be prepared, if we're as close as I think we are, I think Sandi should be brought into the picture, she's going to have to stay indoors for a few days."

"You think, I think, damn, I just wish we could know something for sure for a change!"

"Yeah, well in the meantime you'd better get back to Sandi, stay with her buddy, she's a very special lady, and I don't want her to get hurt."

Sandi finished with the few things she needed to do and decided that she would exercise Rapscallion early, thus leaving herself plenty of time to prepare for dinner. A few days earlier Bill had shown her a path that led through a particularly wooded area just inside the wall bordering the estate. It was rarely used and in places it had become nearly overgrown. There was a peacefulness about it though that attracted her especially today, with her emotions in a turmoil. All morning she had been speculating about the evening that lay ahead, her thoughts battling their own private war within in her mind. On one hand an evening with Steve could be manna from Heaven, on the other hand, it could be sheer hell. She hoped a quiet ride would settle her.

Rapscallion and Bubbles both decided to live up to their names that day. Bubbles bounced and yapped at her feet, nearly tripping her several times before she got her pacified. While Rapscallion decided that he could not stand still for even a second, much less long enough to be saddled. He pranced and pawed and fussed, causing her more than a little aggravation before she succeeded in getting him saddled and bridled. But Sandi smiled satisfactorily as she settled into the saddle, she had not thought of Steve for over twenty minutes, already her plan was working.

A light misty rain began as she turned Rap toward the path, while her thoughts returned to Steve. She shivered slightly glad she had taken the time to change from her light-weight wind-breaker to a heavier coat when she was at her bus saddling Rap.

Her leg brushed against a shrub sending a shower of water onto them from it's water logged leaves. Rapscallion danced away, his hooves making nothing more than soft shuffling sounds on the loamy path. A bird darted up, startled from his perch by their approach, again Rapscallion danced sideways. They moved on, the, stallion becoming tenser and acting more frightened with each passing step; while the path became narrower and darker. Bubbles even seemed unusually alert, flinching at the slightest sound.

Sandi, totally absorbed in her own problems, failed to notice her animal's strange actions at first. It was not until Rapscallion actually shied for the third time in as many minutes, this time because of the narrowness of the trail he bumped her leg on a tree, forcing her to become more aware of her surroundings. The stallion was rarely frightened of anything, even kids setting off firecrackers practically under his nose, had not phased him in the past, so what was the problem now?

She looked around, on a bright and sunny day it was dim and shadowy under the heavy foliage, but on a day such as this one was, already dark and dismal, the light became practically nonexistent. Heavy shadows shrouded everything, creating strange and eerie shapes, and quite suddenly this peaceful haven seemed just the opposite. She

177

felt her panic rise and was completely helpless to stop it. "This is silly," she spoke aloud, trying to break the silence and ease both her own and her horse's fears. "Just calm down and as soon as the path widens a little we'll turn around and go back."

A strange sensation of being watched flooded her senses a few moments later as they came to an area that afforded just enough room for the horse to turn around. Sandi breathed a hearty sigh of relief as she cued Rapscallion to spin; she could not get out of there fast enough.

A sudden pain seared through her left shoulder, its blinding force flinging her forward to lie along the horse's neck. Rapscallion hesitated only a moment before picking up speed, Sandi felt her world spinning, there was another pain in her head now, loud noises assailed her, Bubbles was barking, men were shouting, why was Rap's neck all red? She tried to focus her eyes, but everything changed to a fuzzy black and white, alternating to an image like a photographic negative. She called for Steve, thinking she heard his voice as her horse crashed off the path forging his own trail through the thick wall of under growth, and then she remembered that Steve was not at home.

CHAPTER FIFTEEN

Steve raced across the wide span of grass; never had he felt such terror as at the moment he realized that Sandi was, in fact, El Lobo's next target. The man was a depraved killer with absolutely no regard for life. He was wanted for murder and terrorism in half the countries of the world, and had been for several years. The only problem was, so far no one could catch him and make a charge against him stick. He had more tricks than a magician did and he changed identities like most people change clothes. He was known for one thing, he had never, ever, failed to deliver!

It seemed like an eternity had passed since he had heard the shots, he felt as though he were in slow motion. Bubbles frantic barking suddenly ceased, every agent on the estate was running in the same direction, they all heard the crashing and popping of limbs as Rapscallion crashed through the thick wall of undergrowth. "Please dear God, let her live, please," he prayed as he ran.

Suddenly, Rapscallion broke into the open; he stumbled once, almost losing his precious cargo, before gaining his footing again and racing toward the barn.

The misty fog of darkness lifted slowly, Sandi shook her head, trying to clear it faster, instead sharp knives of pain stabbed at her and the awful darkness threatened to overcome her again. She heard someone speaking to her, but they sounded so muffled, like they were far off in the distance. "Hush darling, it's all over now, just rest, you're going to be fine."

She could have sworn it was Steve, but he wouldn't have called her darling, he wasn't even home, he was never home, he avoided her, it must be Joey, yes, Joey would come to her. "Joey," she whispered softly, just before the dark fog took over her mind again.

It was several hours before Sandi awoke again, the fog seemed to have finally lifted, and the stabbing pains had dulled to throbbing ache, slowly her eyes focused on the antiseptic whiteness around her. She tried to move, but something was holding her down, panic struck with the swiftness of a snake striking down its prey. Where was she, what had happened?

The questions chased through her mind as she began to fight her shackles. Then the smiling face of a nurse appeared within her range of vision.

"Hi there," the nurse spoke cheerfully, "Don't be frightened, you're in the hospital ....You're going to be okay. Do you understand......can you hear me? She asked noting the alarmed expression on Sandi's face.

Sandi was having trouble getting her brain back in gear; nothing seemed to make any sense. Why was she in the hospital?

"What happened, why am I here?' She croaked her throat so dry her voice hardly functioned.

"I'll let the doctor answer that one, he'll be in shortly.,' The nurse told her while checking a conglomerate maze of tubes that Sandi now realized were attached to her own body and the reason that she couldn't move. "If you need anything just press this button." She added, placing a small plastic object in Sandi's hand and closing her fingers around it.

Thoughts bounced around in her mind, dark shadows, Rap running, Bubbles... she felt tired, so very tired, maybe if she slept for awhile things would become clearer.

"Well I think you're going to make it, young lady." the elderly doctor told her when she awoke in the middle of his examination. She opened her mouth to speak, but no sound was forth coming. "Here, have a sip of water, not

181

too much now, you don't want to make yourself sick. I'm Doctor Bradley."

"What happened, why am I here?" She asked as soon as she was able, though her voice sounded more like a frog's croak than her own.

"Don't remember anything, uh?"

She tried, but only fleeting images came to her, being scared, very scared, Rap running, and red, everything was red. She shook her head slowly and carefully, mindful of the pain, "Not really, the last thing I remember clearly was getting on my horse. Was there an accident, did he fall... is he hurt?" She asked quickly, not giving the doctor time in between to answer.

"An accident, no, as I understand it, it was definitely not an accident," he paused, judging whether she was strong enough to take being told the truth just yet, finally deciding she was. "You were shot."

"Shot? Like with a gun... bang, bang? She asked incredulously, realizing too late that she must have sounded nearly as witless as she felt.

The doctor didn't seem to notice. "That's exactly what I mean," He held up his hand, stopping her flood of questions, "I don't know all the whys and wherefores, your husband will return later, he should be able to dot the i's and cross the t's for you. I sent him home to rest this morning, he's been at your side ever since they brought you in," he shook his head, "wouldn't leave until I convinced him you were going to recover. Tell you one thing young lady; don't ever doubt that man's love, I rarely see so much devotion." Sandi was speechless, there had to be some mistake, Steve didn't even want to be near her. Then she recalled a muffled voice saying 'hush darling, it's all over now,, could it really have been Steve?

The doctor continued, not even noticing her lack of attention. "Now then about your injuries, your forehead is bandaged because somehow, probably falling from that horse you say you were on after you were shot. You received a very nasty blow, several stitches and a concussion's worth. You are stiff and sore, because you have numerous contusions... ah, bruises; cuts and scrapes. To put it bluntly my dear, you look like you got into it .with a meat grinder... and you lost."

"That bad?" She asked, smiling, the news that Steve really cared for her overrode anything else he had said, no matter how bad.

"We haven't even discussed the wound from your .... ah, 'bang, bang'," So, she thought ruefully, he had noticed. "I'll try not to bore you with the details. The bullet nicked a large vein near your heart, so there was considerable loss of blood, frankly my dear, I find it a complete miracle that you didn't bleed to death before they got you to the hospital. There was also some damage to your pectoral muscle, nothing permanent, but rather painful. You won't want to use your arm for awhile. And finally," he noticed she was showing signs of tiring, "I want you to stay in the hospital a few more days before we even discuss your release, we'll wait and see how you feel in, let's say three more days. Any questions?"

Sandi shook her head gently, right then all she felt like doing was sleeping. The slightest thing, like holding her eyes open, seemed to wear her out in no time at all. Thinking up the questions would be too much of an effort, much less making her mouth function to ask them. She had drifted back to sleep before the doctor had closed the door behind him.

Steve stood at the foot of Sandi's hospital bed later that afternoon, watching her sleep. Scenes from the terrifying minutes right after she was shot flashed through his mind. The blood drenched stallion standing quivering at

184

the barn door while the motionless body of his mistress laid slumped over his neck. His fingers slipping in her blood while he desperately tried to untangle her hands from the horse's mane. The gaping wound... it was all his fault, how could she ever forgive him, he could never forgive himself.

Sandi's lids fluttered, she saw Steve, and the naked raw pain written in his eyes checked her welcoming smile. "Can you ever forgive me?" He asked; his voice hoarse with emotion.

"What?" Sandi asked, she had no idea of what he was speaking about.

He seemed about to explain, then just shook his head, "I'm sorry," was all he rasped, then he spun around and was gone before she had collected here wits enough to try to stop him.

"Steve," she cried out softly, knowing already that it was too late. He did not return as she had hoped and no amount of worrying or fretting over the next few days brought forth a logical explanation of his behavior either. She learned of what had happened to her when she was shot, in bits and pieces through a series of visitors, of which Sarah and Bill were the first. They both seemed fully convinced that it never would have happened had they not taken the day off and Bill had not shown her the path, so Sandi spent most of their visit convincing them that it could not possibly have made any difference in the way things turned out. She did learn from them that the man who had shot her had somehow been killed while leaving the scene, though they were not sure as to exactly how; and that both her horse and dog had been injured, but not seriously and both were recovering nicely.

Wayne arrived a little later and shed considerably more light on the subject of her assailant. It seemed he was a well known, expert, international assassin that for once had slipped up. Always dropping his victims with only one shot, he had apparently become over confident this time and had carried only a couple of cartridges. Evidently Bubbles went after him right after he fired the first shot, whether he had aimed at her or, the dog with the second shot no one knew, but he had missed. That left him only one defense, flight, which he took, with Bubbles in hot pursuit, right over the six foot block wall surrounding the estate.

"Can you imagine it, right over that wall?" Wayne asked, "Anyway," he continued before she could answer, "she chased him through the gardens of the neighboring estate, out the front gate and straight into the path of an oncoming car. They were both hit, your dog's fine though, she had some internal injuries and a broken leg, but she's healing up and the vet says she'll be good as new real soon." he reassured her. "Unfortunately, your assailant died before we could learn who he was working for."

Nan and her Grandfather visited the next afternoon, completely surprising her when they walked in together. She didn't even know they were acquainted.

"Grandpa!" Sandi cried out with delight when she saw him, "How'd you get here?"

"Plane," he replied with a grin.

Sandi sighed, "That much even I could have figured out, but why...did Steve call you?"

"Nope, as a matter of fact this dear lady did." He indicated Nan, who was standing back giving them a few moments alone, "She invited me to a real fancy dinner party as a surprise for the guest of honor.....incidentally, pardon the pun, but you shot her plans all to hell, I thought I taught you better manners than that."

His lighthearted teasing lifted her sadly sagging spirits, Nan soon joined in and they spent the afternoon visiting. If they were curious about the circumstances surrounding her shooting they refrained from asking, simply accepting things for the way they were and making the best of them. She felt tired but more cheerful and contented than she had in several days when they finally left. Though nothing had been said it was obvious that the two older people were enjoying each other's company immensely, and to Sandi if something good could turn out of her present circumstances it would help to make it all seem a little more worthwhile.

It was Joey, who arrived the following afternoon; that finally shed some light on Steve's strange actions. It seemed that the two of them felt it was their fault she had been shot. He felt so adamantly sorry about it that he spent most of the first few minutes apologizing, over and over and over again. And from every indication Steve felt even more remorseful. As a last ditch effort to flush out the people behind Nash's death and salvage at least a portion of the talks the President was to attend in a few days, Steve had let slip, accidentally on purpose, that Sandi was to attend those talks. They had thought her well enough protected that, any attempt to kidnap her could be thwarted, that, along with the potentiality of catching those involved made it seem like a good idea at the time.

"As it turned out it wasn't such a good idea, we really didn't think they would try to kill you before finding out what was on the real list. The President is trying to find a way to postpone things a little; the talks start the day after tomorrow, but..." Joey let the sentence hang un-ended.

"Well I think the two of you are being prize fools particularly Steve. You both told me it could get pretty hazardous before it was over, as if I couldn't have figured it out on my own, I watched Nash get killed for that stupid list. Steve even told me that I might have to play sitting duck. I don't blame either one of you," she told him seriously, then smiled teasingly. "Things could have been worse, ya know, that idiot could have succeeded in killing me."

"Don't remind me," he groaned, not thinking her comment was even remotely humorous. "I don't think I could have ever faced myself again if that had happened, and I know Steve couldn't. He's been like a mad man these past few days."

"So anyway, you don't know any more now than when I brought you the list?" Sandi asked, quickly changing the subject from the all too touchy one of Steve.

"Yeah, I know that Nash was all over half of New York City before he caught that bus. I'm even pretty sure that he stashed the list somewhere in NYC, the only question is where?"

189

"NYC, New York City?" Sandi asked, a small idea like a light bulb flashed in her mind. "What do you mean, 'all over half of New York City', Joey, tell me what you know?"

"Why?" he asked, completely baffled by her question.

"I promise to explain just as soon as I know if I'm right. Please, Joey tell me,'" she begged.

"Okay," he decided even a long shot was worth a try at this late date. "Let me think... Nash arrived late evening, at Kennedy... from there he took a cab to La Guardia, where he bought a ticket for D.C. Only he never got on the plane, instead he took another cab to a subway station, which I assume he rode for awhile. Anyway, I picked up his trail again about half way across town at another station, where he took another cab to about ten blocks from a bus depot. Whether he walked or caught a cab to the bus depot, I never could find out. All I know is that he bought a ticket and got on the bus that you saw him climb off of at the cafe, you know the rest."

Sandi turned in bed, trying to reach the table beside it, but her arm was so painful that she had to tell him what she wanted. "Hand me that paper and pen over there will you? I think I may know where the list is, or at least a place to start looking. While I figure this out I need you to get, something for me. No questions yet, just get it?" She requested when he started to speak.

Joey nodded his acquiescence. "What'd ya need?"

"A jacket of mine, you know the one, it's light blue, it's oh... a wind breaker."

He nodded, "I know it, I've seen you wear it. It's at home I take it?"

"Actually, it's probably still lying on the bed in my rig. I left it there the day I was shot when I changed into my heavier coat."

He nodded again as he turned and left; hope surging through him, could Sandi possibly know something she hadn't told them? But why had she waited? As had become the usual case of late, nothing was making any sense.

Sandi worked frantically, trying to recall everything on the list as well as several chapters of the cipher book she had been studying. If what she thought was true it could explain a lot. It took most of the time that Joey was gone, but she had discovered the 'what' in the list that had bothered her so much for so long. It did not explain quite

191

as much as she had hoped, in fact, in some ways it created more questions. She read it over again hoping it would make more sense the second time.

> *To he who finds this code*
>
> *Remember all is not as you behold*
>
> *Find another and you will hold*
>
> *The key to secrets to be told*
>
> *Codes in code, keys in key*
>
> *It all begins in NYC*

Joey came in a few moments later, "Found it," he said, tossing the jacket to her.

"Good, see what you make of this," She handed him the paper with the deciphered code written on it, before taking her jacket up and searching through the pockets.

Joey read it through twice before looking up, "Where'd this come from?"

"The list, Let me explain, when the university ran tests on this fabulous memory of mine they also had me do a little studying on ciphers; nothing difficult, just picking out patterns in letters or numbers. Anyway, to make a long story short, the first time I saw the list I picked up on certain patterns. At the time, I only did it to be able to remember it correctly. But later, when I talked to Steve he told me part of what the first line said, the problem was it didn't jive with the pattern I had picked up on earlier, in other words there were two basic patterns. Well, I didn't know what it did say, and I certainly didn't know enough to argue with your experts, so I didn't say anything. Then a few weeks ago, I found a book in Steve's study on ciphers, and just for kicks I started playing around with the list, only I couldn't quite get it figured out, not until today. When you told me about New-York City, NYC, then I put it all together with this," she handed him a small piece of paper that she had found in her jacket pocket. "This is some sort of receipt; it looks like it came from a pawn shop, look at the address on the back, NYC. Apparently, it was in the envelope when Nash gave it to me, it must have fallen out when I took the list out to read it right before hiding it. I found it a couple of weeks ago. I just thought it was a piece of paper that had blown into the tack box or something, so I put it in my pocket to throw it away, only a trash can was never handy when I thought about it, so it just sat there in my pocket. I didn't connect it until today. Joey, why are you looking at me like that, I am on the right track aren't I?"

He shook his head disbelievingly, "I don't believe it, we've had the best people in the agency working on that list, and not one of them picked up on this. I don't know how you did it, but to answer your question, Beautiful, yes, I think you're on the right track,"

CHAPTER SIXTEEN

Sandi did not know that time could drag so slowly, Joey had rushed out saying something; she couldn't quite catch what, about having to call Steve before he left. His words were fired out so fast that Sandi wasn't sure if he meant before Steve left or he himself left for New York. Several questions plagued her incessantly, like what was happening in New York, did they find the list, would the whole thing be settled in a few days so that her life could return to normal, did she even want it to return to normal? Somehow her future didn't look all that bright if Steve wasn't in it, could he possibly love her and what if he didn't?

There was no word from anyone involved with the case. Joey and Steve, she thought, were probably out of town, but even Wayne stayed away. The doctor finally decided she was well enough to be moved into a regular ward where she had a television set. Watching the evening news the following day she discovered that the President was visiting a small country in South America to attend some sort of peace negotiations. In his statement to the press about the first day in the country, the President indicated that things were proceeding very well, in fact, much better than he had hoped. Sandi hoped they really were.

In the local news she learned that someone involved with top secret government work, a major figure in the FBI, was being sought for questioning regarding the sale of said work. His identity had not yet been released to the press so she was left wondering who the double agent was, sure that it must have something to do with the list.

It was rather a shock to see a picture of herself flashed on the screen a few moments later and hear all about her miraculous recovery from several bullet wounds, received in a senseless attack by a terrorist. She had to admit when they replayed a tape of her being taken from the ambulance into the hospital that the amount of blood made it look like there should have been several, but she thought that they should get their facts straight. She did manage to get a quick view of Steve by her side, holding an IV bottle while she was wheeled through the hospital doors, though she hardly recognized him, he looked like he had received a massive blow and was in a state of shock.

The next forty-eight hours proved to be just as frustrating. Her doctor came in late in the afternoon pronouncing her fit enough to empty a much needed hospital bed, providing she agreed to get plenty of rest, not use her arm for anything, and return for a check-up every few days. "I talked to your husband earlier; he said he would make the necessary arrangements. He wants you to be ready about five."

Bewilderment was plainly written on the elderly doctor's face. Her husband had been so attentive at first, now; except for a daily call to him the man seemingly completely ignored his wife. He shook his head; there was just no accounting for people's actions.

Sandi's emotions alternated between 'Sky high and bottom of the ocean low. She wasn't sure how to greet Steve, though aware of and having acknowledged her feelings toward him, she was no closer than ever to knowing what his were for her. As the time passed it seemed as though the minutes started ticking by faster and faster, each second bringing her closer to the time she would again see him and yet no closer to knowing what to say or how to act. By the time the appointed hour arrived her nerves were stretched taut, nearly to a breaking point, so it was almost a relief when Joey walked in.

"Hi beautiful! Are you ready? No questions yet, I'll fill you in on the latest when we're out of here."

"Joey?!" It was a half question, half exclamation. "Wh..."

"Uh-uh, no questions 'til you're out of here."

The nurse came in with a wheel chair insisting that Sandi ride out to the car in it. Sandi had to laugh at that, for the past two days the very same nurse had been insisting that she get out of either the bed or the wheel chair and walk around. Now when she was being sent home, she had to ride out in a wheel chair.

Joey carefully lifted her from the wheelchair to the car, explaining the reason for their sneaking out the back door of the hospital. "Newsmen are stationed out there like a bunch of vultures. I wouldn't be surprised if that's why the hospital is releasing you so soon. Ever since the story broke this morning about you're involvement with the case, they've been hanging around looking for a likely carcass to attack."

"The story? You mean everything was released to the press?"

"Well, not quite everything, just almost," he replied, closing her door and walking around the car.

"Nothing was said about it being the reason for your marrying Steve," he finished while sliding into the driver's seat.

"What story? I haven't heard the news today, what's been going on? I haven't heard a word since you left the other day."

"Then, I think maybe I'd better start at the beginning," he told her while negotiating the car out into the flow of traffic. "Wayne was going to try to stop by and update you but with all that's been going on I guess he hasn't had a chance. Here goes, a day-by-day, blow-by-blow account. Steve and I spent about six hours running frantically around New York piecing the list together. The clue you found was only the first of about a dozen, it was like some ridiculous treasure hunt.

But we found everything finally and in the process discovered that our double agent was non-other than a very trusted employee who worked in the lab. His job was to take in messages from operatives around the world, decode them and turn them over to the proper department. Well, he was very good at his job, only he had this bad habit of occasionally selling little tidbits of information to the other side. A very profitable enterprise, unless of course, you're caught."

"I don't understand, you mean this guy worked at decoding but he never found the hidden message?" Sandi asked.

"Does seem a little strange doesn't it, but you have to remember, nearly everything now is decoded by computers. This guy is more of a computer whiz, than a genius at actually decoding messages. Codes have gotten really complicated since the advent of computers, but a computer only does what the operator tells it to, this guy thought he knew which code Nash was using, and he did decode that which Nash wanted him to. But he never asked the computer to search out another code."

"And no one else did either?"

"That's right. That is really what Nash was banking on, which is what he wanted to tell you to tell Steve to look for the hidden code. He used such an old one that there aren't many people who even remember it, but he knew Steve would, because he had worked on a case with us years ago. Steve and I used to use it to communicate with each other all the time and Steve taught it to Nash."

"So this guy's been caught?"

"He was picked up this morning, along with a gentleman, I use that term loosely known as the Boss, he's the one who almost kidnapped you at the rodeo and there were five or six others, including the woman who called pretending to be a nurse."

"And. now I'm free, my life can return to normal? Well almost," she ruefully acknowledged her arm which hung uselessly in a sling in front of her, "I'll have to make some sort of arrangements until my arm heals. I'm not supposed to drive or lift, etcetera, etcetera, and I'm supposed to see the doctor every few days. I guess when I regain my strength a plastic surgeon is going to do what he can to remove the scar, or at least most of it."

"That's why nothing-was released about your marriage, Steve thought you might like to leave things as they are for awhile." Her hopes soared, only to be quickly dashed as he finished. "He's going to stay in South America for the next three or four weeks so you can have the house all to yourself." He looked over noting her forlorn expression. "What happened between you two anyway? I know it's none of my business, but well, I'd like to help if I can."

"Thanks Joey, but I don't think there's anything you or anyone else can do. He loves someone else, in fact, I think he's still in love with his first wife, but I'm not sure."

"Steve? No way, not his ex, that's for sure, he got over her a long, long, time ago. From the way he's been acting I think he's hooked on you."

"Be serious, oh, I admit he's not immune to me, but that's a far cry from being in love with me."

"What makes you so sure?"

"Oh, a lot of little things really, things he's said, like it wasn't convenient for him to marry me when he had to, and the portrait in his study, stuff like that."

"My dear, it is never convenient for a man to fall in love, and as for the portrait, forget it. That's his ex. He told me one time that he kept it there to remind himself never to make the same mistake again."

"Mistake?" She asked.

"Yep, marriage to that beautiful witch was a definite mistake. You still haven't convinced me that he doesn't love you, but we'll see when he gets back."

"I won't be here when he gets back Joey, I can't, don't you see, I love him, I couldn't face him and then walk away if you're wrong." Tears were welling up and spilling over in her eyes, they had done that quite often lately, she felt so weak and defenseless especially since being shot. "I have to keep a portion of my sanity, I just can't!" She told him angrily, brushing away her tears.

"Okay, okay, just calm down, we don't have to worry about it for a while anyway. And in the mean time I have a favor to ask of you. I know you've been through enough and done enough lately, but this won't take too much effort."

"I haven't done a thing for you and you know it, I haven't even thanked you for all you did for me, somehow words seem a bit inadequate."

"Forget it," he brushed off her comment, "You remember Barbara Parker, the girl you met at the cafe?"

"Of course."

"Well, she's the girl I told you about, and she has finally agreed to marry me."

"Congratulations," try as she might some of the dismay she felt as the thought of Barbara Parker must have shown.

"She's not as bad as you think," he laughed, "I know you two didn't meet under the best of circumstances, but I think if you give her a chance you'll like her. You will give her a chance won't you?"

"Of course, I will," Sandi replied, sincerely hoping he was right.

"Good, because here's the favor, Barb and I want to be married in the gardens at the estate, just as soon as we can get everything arranged. We were hoping you wouldn't mind too much."

"What on earth do I have to do with it? It's not my house and they aren't my gardens, you have to talk to Steve about that." she told him, completely baffled as to why he was asking her, he knew that she wasn't really married to Steve, that it wasn't her place to make those kind of decisions.

"I did ask Steve, he said he didn't mind if that was what you wanted, it was entirely up to you."

"Well, I certainly don't have any objections, in fact I'll help organize it if you'd like." At least it'll give me something to do, she added silently.

"Great, wait 'till I tell Barb," he said as he turned into the estate drive.

CHAPTER SEVENTEEN

Sandi leaned back in the chaise lounge and closed her eyes to block out the burning rays of the mid-day sun. The letter she had just finished reading now lay in her lap fluttering in the breeze. It was not the first time she had read it, in fact she had read it so often that she would have known it by heart, without her gifted memory, but the fact was it didn't make sense, no more this time than all the others. So she kept reading it, trying to understand it.

Joey had given it to her when he brought her home from the hospital that first day, nearly three weeks ago now. He had taken her into the study and retrieved it from the desk, telling her Steve had asked him to give it to her. With shaking hands she had opened the envelope to find the letter and the papers to annul her marriage enclosed. Thinking back on it now she was glad Joey had been with her that day. She had completely broken down and might have done something really stupid had he not been there. It was Joey who had read the letter first; she couldn't bring herself to read his letter after seeing the annulment papers. It was Joey who convinced her that Steve must somehow have the mistaken impression that she and Joey were in love, and it was he, who had convinced her on the basis of the letter to stick around until after Steve returned. He was sure that Steve would be home just as soon as he discovered that Joey was planning on marrying Barbara and not Sandi.

They had decided between them, that the best way to let Steve know was to send him a wedding invitation, it was sent off a couple of days later to the address where he was staying in South America. And then the waiting game began, but now, with the wedding only a few hours away, there had been no word from Steve, and she was sure that there would never be. She had played her hand and lost the game. As she lay there dismal depression washed over her in waves, she felt completely beaten both physically as well as mentally.

The worst part of it was she had nowhere to go now. Only a short while earlier she had received a telegram from her Grandfather telling her of his marriage to Nan the day before in Las Vegas. They had not wished to take any of the limelight away from Joey and Barbara on their special day, so they had slipped quietly off to be married. They would honeymoon on the ranch and hoped Steve and Sandi would visit them when time permitted. So now she couldn't even escape to the ranch to finish recuperating, she wouldn't feel right intruding on them, not now, not so soon after they had found each other, it wouldn't be right.

Well, she thought, I can't very well leave here until after the wedding anyway, Joey has done too much for me to have me walk out and upset his plans at the last minute. She shook her head and shuttered, trying to shake off the depression that had enveloped her. She would just have to make the best of it for a few more hours then she would quietly slip away, with no one the wiser. She knew that her arm had not finished healing, the doctor still didn't want her to drive, but so long as she was careful she wouldn't hurt it, and if she did, she didn't really care, she had to get away!

Steve wasn't sure at first that he had pulled into the right driveway when he arrived a short time later. From the number of cars parked everywhere he realized there must be a hundred or so people at his house. What was going on? He didn't feel very sociable, and if Wayne had not seen him he would probably have turned around and left right then and there. He didn't really care who was using his home for a party or why, he just wanted to be alone. Try as he might to forget her he was still haunted by the memory of Sandi. Knowing that she was with Joey now carried its own special agony, it was a pain that burned his very soul and blocked out the thought of anything else.

Burying himself in his work had not helped, food was tasteless so he ate seldom and very little, sleep was almost nonexistent, and was no real relief, for it was plagued with dreams of Sandi.

Wayne had walked over to his car, "Steve, we didn't think you were going to make it. This will sure make Joey's and Sandi's day, they really want you to be here."

Oh God, he thought, what color he had left drained rapidly from his face, no, they weren't getting married here, not today!

"Hey, you okay? What'd you do, catch a bug down there in the jungle?"

"Must have," he lied, "I sure feel like I caught something." Like a swift kick in the gut, he added to himself, trying desperately to draw on a reserve of strength from somewhere deep inside to steel himself against what he knew he would have to witness.

"Well, come on, they should be about ready to start," Wayne encouraged him.

They had in fact already started with the ceremony by the time Wayne and Steve walked around the house to where the ceremony was taking place. Steve's eyes were riveted to the back of the bride. A pain wretched through him as he watched her kneel in her beautiful long gown and veil at the flower laden alter to receive the minister's blessing, and then she rose and turned to face Joey who lifted the veil to kiss the bride. Barbara! Where was Sandi? Steve's eyes frantically searched the crowd, he couldn't see her. Shock and anger coursed through him, how could Joey do this to her? How could he walk out and leave her for someone else after all she had been through? By God held kill him for this, or at the very least make him wish he were dead!

The couple was coming down the aisle arm in arm, laughing while the crowd congratulated them, when Steve stepped up to Joey, his right arm swung out allowing his fist to connect solidly with Joey's jaw, knocking him back into the crowd.

A few of the women cried out in surprise and shock, while several of the men nearby, including Wayne grabbed Steve and pulled him back when he would have jumped forward and swung again.

"What the hell is going on Steve? Have you lost your mind?" Wayne demanded.

Joey sat up rubbing his jaw, a grin splitting his face despite the pain, for he had known Steve for too long and too well to not know what his friend was thinking. "Not quite, Wayne," he answered for Steve. "It's about time you showed up," he told Steve, "I thought you were going to be too late. You at least ought to give me a chance to explain." Steve was beginning to get control of his temper. He nodded slightly. "Let him go," Joey told the men who had grabbed Steve. "If you'll come into your study where we can talk in private I'll explain a few things to you. Then he turned to Barbara who was now kneeling over him with concern, "Take care of the guests will you Hon, I'll be back in a couple of minutes, it's alright," he added when she looked skeptically from him to Steve.

"Start explaining!" Steve spun around to face him and commanded as soon as Joey closed the door of the study behind them a few minutes later. "Explain how you could do this to Sandi!"

Joey calmly walked over the desk and picked up an envelope, handing it to Steve.

Steve ripped it open, eyeing Joey with animosity. Several small pieces of paper fluttered to the floor. Those are you're annulment papers in case you're interested. I couldn't marry Sandi even if I wanted to, it's against the law in this country."

Steve looked from him to the papers and back again incredulously, "She tore them up?" he asked dumbfounded.

"She's in love with you," Joey side stepped the question.

Steve still couldn't believe it, "She loves me, and she tore up the papers?"

"Actually I did," Joey finally admitted, "but she does love you, I can promise you that, she thinks that you don't give a damn about her, and she's out there right now getting ready to-load up her horse and pull out. If you don't get out there and stop her it's going to be too late." The last part of his sentence was received by empty space; Steve had turned and ran from the room.

CHAPTER EIGHTEEN

"Put that horse away!" Steve ordered as Sandi appeared at the stall door leading Rap.

"Steve?" Sandi looked up in surprise, not really believing her ears or her eyes.

"You, my beautiful wife, are not going anywhere. Not until we have talked at any rate," he told her sternly.

She eyed him suspiciously, why was he here? Why was he looking at her that way? Why now? If he cared so much about her, why had he waited so long to come home? "We have nothing more to say to one another." She told him quietly.

Steve moved forward, a quiet forcefulness about him. "You think not, I can think of several things, starting with this," he swept her unceremoniously into his arms, his lips crushing hers with a passion turned nearly violent from suppressed passion; a passion that lit the fires of her own to send it scorching through her veins. Her body, arched forward against his sinewy male frame, her own needs matching his as their souls meshed. Slowly his kisses softened, becoming gentle and teasing as his lips burned a path from her mouth along her jaw to her ear, leaving her body clamoring for fulfillment.

"I love you," he whispered, trying to break himself free from her drugging force so they could talk. There had been too much misunderstanding, for too long. "I love you so much it hurts, so much that I would have let you go to Joey if that was what you wanted."

"Whatever made you think I wanted Joey? I love you I think I have since the first day I met you," her eyes told him more than mere words could ever say. They virtually shone with love for him. "I thought you were in love with the girl in the portrait."

"We've been fools," he groaned holding her away from him, looking at her as if literally drinking her in.

Rapscallion had never been able to stand being completely ignored, as he was at the moment. Thinking he had been patient with this program long enough, he nudged Sandi with his nose in her back, pushing her into Steve's more than willing arms. "You've got the right idea Rap, keep it up boy." Steve laughed at the horse. "Now will you put him away?" He asked her, "If I hold you like this much longer I will not be held responsible for my actions and there are several things we need to discuss?"

Sandi backed Rap into the stall and removed his halter, returning to Steve's arms as quickly as she could.

"I never again want to go through what I have the last few weeks," he told her, holding her close again, "first thinking I'd gotten you killed, then having to watch a wedding where I thought you were marrying my best friend."

"What do you mean, watching me marry your best friend? We never did figure out how you got the idea I loved Joey. But I thought you knew they were getting married. Didn't you get the invitation to their wedding?"

Steve shook his head, "What invitation?"

"When Joey brought me home from the hospital we read your letter, he was convinced that you thought we were in love, so he sent you an invitation to their wedding. He was sure that you would come home just as soon as you read it. When you didn't come, I thought it was because you didn't care." A single tear rolled down her cheek.

He kissed her gently, licking the tear from her face. "He was right you know, I would have come, but I never got it. It's probably laying in some post office in South America somewhere, I came home thinking you would be gone and I could, go quietly insane all by myself, with only your memories to keep me company. Only when I got here there were cars everywhere, I was just leaving when Wayne caught me, let me see, what'd he say, something about how happy you and Joey would be that I'd made it. When I saw the bride, whom I thought was you, I almost stopped the wedding, then Joey lifted the veil and there was Barbara standing there.

"So then you knew?"

"Oh no, then I knew I would kill Joey for hurting you," he flexed his fingers, "that boy has a very hard jaw."

"Steve you didn't?" her eyes opened wide with horror.

"I did, and I would have hit him again if I hadn't been held back, you know" he laughed, "thought it was real funny," Steve smiled, "guess it is in a way. Anyway, he took me into the study and explained a few facts. Like you were still my wife, and that you loved me," he bent his head and kissed her gently again, "Of course; I'm still going to need a lot of convincing." he whispered with his lips only a fraction of an inch from hers.

It was a long time before they returned to the party, in fact Joey and Barbara were just getting ready to leave.

I probably should apologize, but if you're half as happy as I am at the moment you wouldn't hear me anyway." Steve told him, reaching out to shake Joey's hand. "Congratulations guy."

"You too, and no apologies are necessary, so long as you take good care of her."

'Never fear, this is one lady I'm never going to let go of again. She's mine!" he growled, pulling Sandi close with his arm around her waist.

Steve and Sandi stood arm and arm watching the last guest leave later that evening. "Well, Mrs. Hoyt, do you think you can leave the cleaning up to the maid this time, and come up to bed with your husband?"

"What? No night cap," Sandi asked in mock horror as she slipped from his grasp and raced laughing up the stairs with Steve in hot pursuit.

END

Printed in the USA
CPSIA information can be obtained
at www.ICGtesting.com
LVHW010427190524
780579LV00013B/524